TO CATCH A KILLER

"Jesus," Clint said when Spender lifted the blanket to show the girl to him. He had to swallow hard; he had seen some gruesome things in his life—but nothing like this. The fact that the girl was so young made it even worse.

"It looks messy," Clint said, "but the cut looks neat."

"Sharp knife."

"And somebody knew what they were doing."

"A doctor?"

Clint nodded.

"Jesus," Spender said. "Doctors are supposed to save lives, aren't they?"

"Most of them do," Clint said.

"How many don't?"

Clint looked down at the girl's body, shook his head, and said, "At least one, I guess."

THE GUNSMITH

218

THE CLEVELAND CONNECTION

J. R. ROBERTS

JOVE BOOKS, NEW YORK

THE CLEVELAND CONNECTION

A Jove Book / published by arrangement with
the author

PRINTING HISTORY
Jove edition / February 2000

The Penguin Putnam Inc. World Wide Web site address is
http://www.penguinputnam.com

ISBN: 0-515-12756-6

A JOVE BOOK®
Jove Books are published by The Berkley Publishing Group,
a division of Penguin Putnam Inc.,
375 Hudson Street, New York, New York 10014.
JOVE and the "J" design
are trademarks belonging to Penguin Putnam Inc.

PRINTED IN THE UNITED STATES OF AMERICA

10 9 8 7 6 5 4 3 2 1

THE GUNSMITH
218
THE CLEVELAND CONNECTION

PROLOGUE

Clint looked to his right and saw George Karl coming up alongside him. Karl was the railroad detective whose work had led them to this place. Other than Talbot Roper, Heck Thomas, and James Hume, Karl was the best detective Clint had ever seen.

"Okay," Karl said, "they're inside."

"All of them?" Clint asked.

"All five."

"And how many men have we got?"

Karl looked at Clint and said, "You and me."

"What happened to your other men?"

"To tell you the truth, Adams," Karl said, "I think they got lost."

Clint looked down at the outlaws' hideout, a small shack in the middle of nowhere with not much cover around it.

"I don't think we can afford to wait for them to find us, do you?" Clint asked.

"No," Karl said, "we've got to hit them while they're inside. If we let them get out it's us against them out in the open."

"Agreed," Clint said. He looked at Karl's rifle. "I know you're a good detective, but can you hit anything with that?"

"Only whatever I point it at."

"Okay," Clint said. "I'll make my way down to the shack while you cover me."

"Wait a minute," Karl said. "I got you into this, and it's my job, not yours. You stay up here and cover me. I *know* you can shoot."

"You're a little stockier than I am, George."

"You saying I'm fat?"

Clint looked George Karl up and down. The man was just stocky, just this side of tending toward fat. Clint felt sure that in another eight or ten years George Karl probably would be very fat. But whatever happened, at the moment the railroad detective was not exactly fleet of foot.

"I'm saying I'm faster on my feet than you are, George," Clint said. "Are you going to argue that with me?"

Karl thought a moment, then said, "No."

"Good," Clint said. "Then I'll go down there and get as close as I can to the house. With any luck I can be back up against one side of it. When I do that, it's your turn to come down, and I'll cover you."

"Okay."

"If that door opens while I'm out in the open," Clint said, "you'll have to shoot whoever comes out."

"Don't worry," Karl said. "I will."

"Okay then, good luck."

"Don't step in any chuckholes."

Clint gave Karl a look and said, "That's a hell of a thing to say," and started down the hill.

Inside the house Jake McCandles and his gang were sitting around a table arguing over their next move.

"I think we're done with the railroads, Jake," Ted Shipley said.

"Who says you get to make that decision?" McCandles demanded.

"I ain't makin' a decision, Jake," Shipley said, "I'm just givin' my opinion."

"I ain't asked for your opinion; have I?" McCandles asked. He looked around at the other three men, Bud Spencer, Jake's brother Ike and the Rat man, Bill Porter. He was called the Rat man because they often made money betting on how many rats he could kill without using his hands—just his teeth.

"Anybody else got an opinion?" Jake asked.

"Nope," Spencer said. The Rat man just shook his head. Ike didn't say a word. He always supported Jake's decisions.

"So I'll say when we're finished with the railroads," Jake said. "There's still money to be made robbing trains."

"But they got George Karl after us now," Shipley said.

"Karl's just another railroad detective, Ted."

"He's a damn good one," Shipley said. "He coulda tracked us here."

"Nobody tracked us here," Jake said, "but just to ease your mind . . . Ike, why don't you go outside and have a look? Put our friend Ted's mind at ease, huh?"

"Sure, Jake."

Ike McCandles got up from his chair, loosened his gun in his holster and headed for the door.

Clint was halfway down the hill, his body angled for easy descent. This meant that he could not see the front door of the shack. George Karl saw it, had a bead on it with his rifle, and as it opened he knew what he was going to have to do. His shot would cover Clint Adams, alert him . . . and probably save his life.

When Ike McCandles came walking out the door he saw the dust cloud Clint Adams was kicking up as he came down the hill. He shouted and went for his gun at the same time.

George Karl fired.

Later, after all hell broke loose and then calmed down again, Clint and Karl started to walk among the bodies.

They both paused to look down at the dead man who had scars all over his face from rat bites.

"It's amazing he didn't die a long time ago from one of those bites," Karl said. "Rats carry disease, man!" He was speaking to the dead man, who was beyond hearing him.

They both heard horses and turned to have a look. It was the rest of Karl's men, finally arriving.

"Dead weight," Karl said, shaking his head.

"That was a hell of a shot, George," Clint said, putting his hand out for the railroad man to shake. "Saved my life."

"You saved my bacon backing me up here, Clint," Karl said. "If there's ever anything I can do for you, you let me know."

"Same here," Clint Adams said. "I owe you for that shot."

"Come on," Karl said. "Least the rest of these losers can do it account for the dead. Let's get back to Denver and I'll buy you a drink."

"Suits me."

ONE

Clint Adams had never been to Cleveland, Ohio, before. All he knew about it was that it was smaller than New York and Philadelphia, slightly smaller than San Francisco, but larger than one of his favorite cities, Denver.

As he stepped off the train he thought about the last time he had seen George Karl. It had been in Denver, about ten years ago, when Karl was still working for the Pacific Coast railroad line. In fact, as a result of having rounded up the McCandles gang Karl had just been made Chief Detective.

Clint had lost track of George Karl since then until a telegram arrived in Labyrinth, Texas, asking him to come to Cleveland. Karl's telegram did not mention that there was still a debt between them, but Clint knew that without having to be reminded of it.

He looked both ways on the platform in the train station and saw a uniformed policeman approaching from his left.

"Mr. Adams?" The policeman was young, his uniform new. Clint could tell by the shine on his buttons, and on his badge. They matched the shine on his shoes.

"That's right."

"I'm Officer Hedges, sir," the young man said. "I'm to

escort you to the Saxon Hotel, the finest hotel in Cleveland."

"Is that a fact?"

"Yes, sir, it is."

"I was supposed to be meeting a friend of mine," Clint said, "George Karl. Do you know him?"

"Yes, sir," the officer said. "That's who sent me to fetch you."

"I see."

"Do you have luggage?"

Clint looked down at the old carpetbag he was holding and said, "Just this."

"A horse?"

"I didn't bring my horse."

"Well, I have a buggy waiting out front," Officer Hedges said. "If you'll follow me?"

"Sure thing, Officer," Clint said. "Lead the way."

Clint thought that whatever George Karl was doing in Cleveland must have been pretty important for him to be able to supply a police escort for him from the train station to his hotel.

The best hotel in Cleveland.

"Here you are," Hedges said, as they pulled up in front of a very impressive-looking four-story hotel. "The Saxon. It's the most modern hotel in the city."

"I can see that," Clint said, as he stepped down from the buggy.

"Shall I take you inside, sir?" Hedges asked.

"I think you've done enough, Officer," Clint said. "I can take it from here. Checking in shouldn't be a problem."

"No, sir," Hedges said. "You're all checked in. Just stop at the desk and they'll give you a key."

"See? I really don't need your help, at all."

"Yes, sir," the man said. "I can see that. Enjoy our city, sir."

"Wait a minute," Clint said. "When will I be seeing Mr. Karl?"

"Oh," the Officer said, because he'd obviously forgotten something. "I was supposed to tell you that there will be a message waiting for you at the desk."

"All right, then," Clint said. "Thanks for the lift, Officer."

"Sir," Hedges said, and got back into the buggy, which drove away.

Clint walked to the door of the hotel where a doorman held it open for him.

"Have a good day, sir," he said.

"Thanks."

The lobby was ostentatious, to say the least. High-ceilinged, with lots of crystal and shiny floors that almost looked wet. He walked to the front desk and put his bag down.

"Can I help you, sir?" the desk clerk asked. He was a well-dressed young man with incredibly pale skin, not a hint of beard stubble, and soft-looking hands.

"I understand there's a room waiting for me."

"And your name, sir?"

"Clint Adams."

"One moment." The clerk checked a book and then smiled brightly at Clint. "There is indeed a room for you, Mr. Adams. Would you like help with your bag?"

"No, that's fine," Clint said. "I've just got the one."

"Here's the key," the clerk said, handing it to him. "Your room is on the second floor, sir, in the front. One of our very best rooms. You can take the elevator, if you prefer to."

Clint had been in elevators before, and while they didn't exactly scare him, he said, "What about the stairs?"

"Well, yes sir, you can take the stairs if you like. Just turn right at the top."

"Thank you." Clint picked up his bag, then stopped. "Oh, yes, is there a message for me?"

"I'll check." The clerk turned, took a slip of paper from

one of the cubbyholes behind him. "Yes, sir, there is. I'm sorry I didn't give it to you right away."

"No problem," Clint said. He looked at the envelope with his name printed on the front, decided to read it in his room. He slipped it into his pocket.

"Right at the top of the stairs, you said?"

"Yes, sir."

"Okay, thanks."

"Enjoy your stay, sir."

"I will."

Clint walked to the stairs and took them to the second floor. He turned right at the top and walked down a very wide hallway until he found the room number that corresponded with the number on the key. He unlocked the door and walked inside. The room matched the promise of the lobby. It was huge, with overstuffed furniture in dark shades of maroon, and heavy curtains to match on the windows. There was no bed, though. That was in a second room, which was almost as big. There was a chest of drawers, another overstuffed armchair, a contraption to hang jackets on, and a large closet filled with hangers.

Whatever George Karl was doing in Cleveland it looked as if he'd really stepped in it.

TWO

The note was from George Karl and it instructed Clint to be down in the dining room at eight P.M. for dinner. Since he knew he was traveling to a "city" and not a "town" Clint had packed accordingly. Not only had he brought more dressy trousers and shorts than he was used to wearing—except when in San Francisco, Denver, or New York—but he had also brought his little Colt New Line, because it wouldn't do for him to be walking down the city streets wearing his western rig. He had never taken to wearing a shoulder holster, though, so whenever he wore the New Line he just tucked it into his belt in the back, so that it nestled there in the small of his back.

Presentably dressed for the kind of dining room the Saxon Hotel would obviously have—he hoped—he left his room and went back downstairs just two hours after he had arrived and presented himself at the doorway of the dining room.

As he'd expected the dining room was magnificent, matching the lobby perfectly. A well dressed white haired man approached him and asked, "Can I help you, sir? Are you a guest of the hotel?"

"Yes, I am, but I'm also meeting someone."

"And who would that be, sir?"

"A Mister George Karl?"

"But of course," the man said. "Please follow me and I will escort you to his table."

"Thank you."

He hadn't seen George Karl in ten years, but he recognized him immediately. His prediction about the man had come true. Karl looked as if he weighed fifty pounds more than he had when they last saw each other, but Clint was still able to recognize him. As they approached the table Karl stood up and smiled expansively.

"Clint, goddamn!" he said, sticking his hand out.

The two men shook hands warmly. Ten years had not lessened the fondness they'd felt for each other after the McCandles affair.

"George, it's good to see you."

"And not hard to see me, huh?" Karl said, slapping his sides. "Remember when I accused you of accusing me of being fat?"

"I remember."

"Come on, have a seat," Karl said. He waved his arm and a waiter appeared. "Andrew, bring Mr. Adams a glass of wine."

"Beer will be fine, George," Clint said.

"Make that beer, Andre. Is steak still your favorite?" Karl asked.

"It is."

"Good. Andre, a huge steak with a lot of onions and plenty of blood."

"Yes, sir. Right away."

As the waiter left, Karl sat back in his chair with a sigh.

"Damn, it's good to see you."

"You too, George. I'm guessing you're not with the railroad anymore?"

"You guess right," Karl said. "Left them two years ago. I was still chief detective, but going nowhere fast."

"So you came here."

"Had a job offer I couldn't turn down."

"I'll bet it's a good one. Are you really paying my bill here?"

"Let's say it's being taken care of."

"By who?"

"Well, I guess technically speaking, by that man at the corner table."

Clint looked at the table Karl was indicating, There was a huge man—much fatter than Karl himself who, by comparison, was simply big—sitting across from a lovely woman with chestnut hair and a low-cut gown showing off an impressively deep cleavage.

"And who might he be?"

"That is our mayor, Hiram Morgan."

"The mayor is paying my bill?"

"Well, sort of," Karl said. "Actually, it's being taken care of by the city."

"And who is that woman?" Clint asked, having barely heard his friend.

"Ah, that is Miss Grace Abbott, a very accomplished stage actress who has come to Cleveland for several performances. Maybe you'll get a chance to see her while you're here."

Clint looked at Karl.

"And how long am I going to be here, George?"

"We don't have to talk about that now, Clint. Here comes your beer. Let's drink to friendship."

As Andrew set Clint's beer down in front of him Clint said, "I'm always ready to drink to friendship, George."

"Good, then here's to it."

Karl lifted his glass of wine and Clint his beer and they drank.

"When did wine become your drink of choice?" Clint asked.

"Just with dinner," Karl said, setting his glass down. "I still enjoy a glass of beer before and after."

"I'm very impressed with this hotel, George," Clint said, "and with Cleveland. I've never been here."

"Did you see much of it?"

"Just during the ride from the station to here."

"We're very proud of our harbor, at the mouth of the Cuyahoga River, and we'll have to get you out on Lake Erie while you're here."

"A ride on the lake, a night at the theater," Clint said. "Sounds like you have big plans for me."

Karl regarded Clint quietly for a few moments, then said, "If you agree to help me you'll probably be here for a while."

"What's a while?"

"I guess that depends on how well we work together."

"We worked together pretty well ten years ago."

"A lot's changed since then," Karl said. "For one thing, I'm not as mobile as I used to be."

"You were never very mobile, as I remember."

"You were faster than me," Karl said, "that's all I ever admitted to."

"Come on, George," Clint said, "give. What are you doing here? Have you gone private? Do you have your own detective agency? Challenging old Allan Pinkerton?"

"Not quite," Karl said. "I'm in law enforcement, Clint."

"You're a policeman?" Clint asked. "That's why a policeman met me at the station."

"Not really," Karl said. "You see, I'm the police commissioner, Clint, and I need you to help me keep my job."

"How am I supposed to do that?"

"By helping me catch a killer."

THREE

"Wait a minute," Clint said. "You're the police commissioner?"

"That's right."

"Is that like the chief of police?"

"No," Karl said. "There's a chief of police, and a chief of detectives, but they both report to me."

"So you're in charge of the whole police department?"

"That's right."

"And who do you report to?"

Karl inclined his head toward the mayor's table and said, "To the man who hired me."

"So you have an entire police department at your disposal and you want me to help you catch a killer?"

"That's right."

"George, I don't understand," Clint said. "For one thing, I'm not a detective."

"I've been following your career, Clint," Karl said. "New York? Denver? Hell, London, England? You've caught your share of killers."

"Maybe so," Clint said, "but I'm no detective."

"I'm gonna tell you something, and some friends of yours agree with me," Karl said.

"Who?"

"Tal Roper, for one. Heck Thomas, another."

"Agree about what?"

"You're the most natural-born detective I ever met."

"That's hogwash—".

"It's true."

"You're trying to get me to agree—"

"I am trying to get you to agree to help me," Karl said, "but it's *because* you're a natural."

"George, listen—"

"Here comes our dinner," Karl said. "Let's eat and talk about it later, huh?"

Clint was about to object but then Andrew put down in front of him the most beautiful steak dinner he'd ever seen.

"Okay," he said, "you got a deal."

"Who is that man sitting over there?" Grace Abbott asked the mayor of Cleveland.

"Where, my dear?"

"There, in the center of the room."

"Oh, that is my police commissioner, George Karl."

"The big man?"

"Yes."

"I'm referring to the other man; the one seated with him."

"Oh," Hiram Morgan said, miffed that someone was taking this lovely creature's attentions away from him, "I'm afraid I don't know who that is. He's a stranger to me. Probably just a friend of the commissioner's. Why?"

"No reason," she said. "He just . . . looks interesting."

"Let's talk about what you will be doing after your premier tomorrow night . . ." Morgan said.

Not only was the steak beautiful, but it was delicious, as well.

"If you're depending on the food to keep me here you're

going to win," Clint said, as he finished his last bite.

"I'm only depending on you wanting to stay and help me, Clint," George Karl said. "I'm not using any tricks, and I'm not going to pull out any old debts."

"I owe you a big one, you know."

"I know," Karl said, "and I owe you one. They should probably cancel each other out."

"It doesn't work that way, George, and you know it."

Clint looked over at the mayor's table and caught the actress, Grace Abbott, looking his way again—or she caught him looking hers. Whichever it was, their glances were heating up the air between them.

"I do know that, Clint," Karl said. "I know it very well. I just want you to know I'm not using that here."

"Then what are you going to use?" Clint asked.

"The facts," Karl said.

"What are the facts?"

"The one irrefutable fact is, if I don't catch this killer soon I'm going to lose my job."

"Have you been told that?"

"Not in so many words," Karl said, "but the implication is plain."

"Is there someone waiting in the wings for your job?"

"Oh, yes," Karl said. "I have very ambitious men working under me. Both my chiefs want my job."

"Could they be sabotaging the search for this killer to get you fired?"

"They could," Karl said. "I wouldn't put it past them."

"So you can't trust them."

"No."

"Is there anyone in the department you can trust? You must have a lot of other men."

"I do, but some of them are loyal to the chief of detectives, and some are loyal to the chief of police."

"And some are loyal to you?"

"There are only a few I'm dead sure of."

"Like the young one you sent to the train station to pick me up?"

"Yes, like him, and a few like him."

"Any experienced men?"

"One or two."

"What about you, George?"

"What about me?"

"You're one of the best detectives I've ever known," Clint said. "What about you?"

"I don't get around as much as I used to, Clint," Karl said. "I can't get out there in the streets and do what I have to do. You can."

"I don't know these streets, George."

"The few men I can rely on do. They'll help you. I'll make it official. You'll be a special agent reporting only to me."

"With a badge?"

"If you want."

"I don't want a badge."

"I'll give you one," Karl said. "You can carry it, you don't have to wear it."

"George—"

"Clint, take tonight to think it over, will you? That's all I ask."

Clint looked over at the mayor's table again. This time the woman's look was almost beseeching. It said, "Save me."

"Do you have to clear this with the mayor?"

"I will have to, yes," Karl said, "but he'll clear it."

"Are you sure? If he wants you out—"

"He wants the killer caught, first and foremost. He'll let me do whatever I have to in order to get it done."

"All right," Clint said.

"You'll do it?"

"I'll think about it, like you asked," Clint said, "but I want one thing tonight."

"What's that?"

"I want to meet the mayor."

"You got it," Karl said. "Let's go over there right now and I'll introduce you."

FOUR

As they approached the table Clint could see that the mayor would have trouble if he attempted to stand. He hoped he wouldn't, because he might take the whole table with him.

Grace Abbott looked up at the two approaching men and her smile already said, "thank you," to Clint.

Mayor Morgan saw the two men approaching and scowled. He didn't want his dinner interrupted, or his evening with the lovely Miss Abbott. He was desperately trying to figure out a way to get her to go to bed with him.

"Don't get up, Mr. Mayor," Karl said as they reached the table, "I just want you to meet a friend of mine. Mayor Hiram Morgan, this is Clint Adams."

The mayor's scowl turned to a look of surprise. He extended a pudgy hand to Clint, who shook it as briefly and as politely as he could.

"Mr. Adams," Morgan said, "I know your reputation, sir. What brings you to Cleveland?"

"Well, as George said, Mr. Mayor," Clint answered, "we're friends. I hadn't seen him in a while, and I've never been to Cleveland."

"Well, I hope you'll like our city," the mayor said. "We're very proud of it."

"I'm sure I will," Clint said, and looked pointedly at

Grace Abbott. This close—and from this angle—her cleavage looked even deeper and more impressive, as did her violet eyes and lovely, full-lipped mouth.

"Oh, forgive my manners, gentlemen," Morgan said. "Miss Grace Abbott, the famous stage actress, this is our police commissioner George Karl, and his friend, Mr. Clint Adams."

"Delighted to meet both of you gentlemen," Grace Abbott said.

"The pleasure is all ours, ma'am," Clint said.

"Won't you join us for a drink?" she asked, her eyes pleading with Clint to accept.

"Oh, I don't think we should—" Karl started to say, but Clint interrupted him.

"We'd like that very much," Clint said, "as long as it's all right with the mayor?" He looked at Mayor Morgan.

"Of course," the mayor said, magnanimously, "please join us."

Since it was a table for four that was easily accomplished. Clint went around to the other side of the table, so he would be able to see the entire room from there. He'd been very uncomfortable at the table in the center of the room. Now he was sitting with Grace Abbott to his right and the mayor to his left. George Karl sat directly across from him.

Andrew, the waiter, seeing that the two of them had joined the mayor and his guest, hurried over.

"Andrew," Mayor Morgan said, "some wine for our guests."

"Clint might prefer beer—" Karl started, but Clint interrupted him once again.

"Wine will be fine, George," Clint said, looking at Grace Abbott. "After all, this is sort of a special occasion."

Karl and Morgan exchanged a glance while Clint and Grace Abbott looked at each other, and both men sort of shrugged.

FIVE

"Tell me, Mr. Adams," Grace Abbott said, "what is this reputation the mayor referred to?"

"It's nothing much," Clint said.

"Nothing?" the mayor said. "Why, my dear, this is the infamous Clint Adams, also known as the Gunsmith. Surely you've heard of his exploits back East?"

"Oh, of course!" Grace said. "I simply didn't connect his real name." She looked at Clint with even more interest than before. "How wonderful to meet such a legendary figure of the old West. I never expected that it would happen in Cleveland."

"Cleveland," Mayor Morgan said, "will surprise you, my dear."

"It already has, Mr. Mayor," she said. "It already has."

They talked awhile over wine, Grace explaining that she was in Cleveland to perform Shakespeare.

"*Macbeth*," she said. "One of my favorite plays." She put her hand on Clint's arm. "Perhaps you and the commissioner will be able to come and see me perform one night?"

"If it's at all possible," Clint said, "we will be there every night."

21

"Well," she said, "I only hope that I am worthy of such support."

"I'm sure you will be."

"If I am to be," she said, "then I must take my leave. I'll need my beauty sleep if I'm to appear on stage without shadows under my eyes."

"But, my dear," Mayor Morgan said, "it's so early."

"I'm sorry, Mr. Mayor," she said, "but I really must get some rest."

"I'll see you to the door then, and get you a cab." The mayor started to slide out from beneath the table.

"Oh, it won't be necessary for you to get up," Grace said. "I'm sure Mr. Adams can see me to the door."

"I'd be delighted to," he said.

Clint stood up and extended his hand to Grace. She put hers into his and he helped her to her feet, then tucked her hand into the crook of his arm.

"It was nice meeting you, Commissioner. Mr. Mayor, I'll be seeing you tomorrow night, at the opening?"

"Uh, yes, yes," the mayor said, "of course."

"I'll be right back, gents," Clint said, and walked Grace Abbott away from the table and out of the dining room.

Morgan and Karl looked at each other briefly, and then Morgan asked, "What's he doing here, George?"

"Like he said," Karl replied, "he came to visit me. We haven't seen each other in years."

"Well," Morgan said, "if that's true, and he is here by coincidence, I hope you plan to try to press him into service."

Karl saw his opening. "Press him into—oh, you mean get him to help find the killer?"

"Of course that's what I mean."

"Well, he's really not a detective, sir—"

"If he agrees to help," Morgan said, "and we can say so in the newspaper, it might just scare this killer away—or at least worry him enough that he might make a mistake."

"Oh, I don't know," Karl said. "Even if he agrees to help

I don't think he'd want us to release it to the newspapers."

"That's okay," Morgan said, "it could *leak* out, somehow."

"I might have to give him some official status."

"Give him what he wants, George," Morgan said. "Pay for his damn hotel, give him a badge, but get him to agree."

"Yes, sir," George Karl said, "I'll try my best," thinking that this had been much easier than he'd imagined.

Out in the lobby Grace Abbott said, "It took you long enough. I was sending help messages to you since you sat down."

"I'm sorry," Clint said. "It took me a little while to interpret them. George wanted to keep talking to me."

"Well, no matter," she said. "You finally came and rescued me, and for that I will be forever grateful. The mayor is a nice enough man, but he is so boring . . . and he undressed me with his eyes."

"You can't fault him for *that*, anyway."

She laughed and said, "Perhaps not, but I truly think he expected to get me into bed tonight." She shuddered at the thought.

As they reached the door Clint asked the doorman to get a cab for the lady.

"Where would you like to go, ma'am?" the doorman asked.

"The Roberts Hotel."

"Yes, ma'am."

"It's a nice hotel," she said to Clint, "but nothing like this."

"This, I've been told," Clint said, "is the finest, most modern hotel in the city."

"I would love to get a look at one of these rooms sometime."

"I'm sure that could be arranged . . . by the mayor," Clint said.

"Your cab is ready, ma'am," the doorman said, sticking his head in the door.

"I'll be right there." She looked at Clint. "So, shall I expect you tomorrow night to the opening?"

"I hope so," Clint said. "It will depend on what George has in store for me."

"Well," she said, "hopefully I can count on you to come at least one night, after that brash promise to come every night."

"It's a promise I firmly hope to keep," Clint said. He took her hand and kissed it gently.

"Good," she said. "I'll hold you to it. Good night, Mr. Adams, and once again, thank you for the rescue."

"Good night, Miss Abbott."

He waited until her cab had driven away, and then turned and walked back to the dining room.

SIX

When Clint reentered the dining room he noticed that the mayor was deep in conversation with George Karl. In fact, the mayor was doing most of the talking. This looked like more than just a social conversation.

Morgan was leaning heavily on the table, speaking earnestly to Karl, and when he saw Clint returning he leaned back in his chair and assumed a more pleasant expression.

"A lovely lady," Clint said, seating himself.

"And talented," Morgan said. "We were very lucky to get her, indeed. I hope you'll be able to attend the play, Mr. Adams. We're very proud of our theater."

"I'll try, Mayor. I guess that will depend on how long I'm going to be here," Clint replied.

"Yes, of course," the mayor said. "Well, it's time for me to go, but please, both of you stay and have another drink. I'll take care of the bills for both your table and mine."

"That's very generous of you, Mayor," Clint said.

"Not at all."

The man struggled to get up without upsetting the table and, remarkably, was successful.

"It was a pleasure to meet you, Mr. Adams. I do hope your stay in Cleveland will be a long one."

"Thank you, sir."

As the mayor walked away Clint said, "He didn't say he hoped it would be a pleasant one."

Karl didn't reply.

"Why didn't he wish me a pleasant stay, George?"

"Well—and this was his idea—he wants me to ask you to stay and help me catch the killer."

"His idea?"

"I didn't have a chance to bring it up."

"Wait a minute," Clint said. "You were going to pay my bill here, weren't you?"

"Only if I couldn't get him to," Karl said, "but he offered. He told me to give you whatever you wanted to get you to stay and help."

"Why? Why does he want me to stay? Does he know I'm not a detective?"

"He knows that."

"I get it," Clint said. "He wants my name, right? He thinks my name will scare the killer away?"

"He hopes," Karl said. "I don't believe he really thinks that any more than I do. This killer is not going to scare, Clint."

Clint hesitated a moment, then said, "I don't like being used, George."

"I don't want to use you, Clint," Karl said. "I mean, I do want to use you, but not like that . . . Look, just do what you said you'd do, okay? Think it over and let me know tomorrow. I'll meet you here for breakfast."

"Fine," Clint said. He might as well get a night in a beautiful hotel out of it, and another meal, even if he decided not to stay and help.

"How about another drink?" Karl asked.

"Sure," Clint said, "but make it a beer this time."

SEVEN

Dr. Henry Cecil watched as his assistant, Dimitri, locked the door to his surgery, checking to make sure it was quite secure. Dimitri was a big man, and if he could not budge the door, no one else would be able to.

"It is secure, Doctor," the big man said.

"Good. Did you get the buggy ready?"

"Yes, sir."

"Excellent. And are you armed?"

"Yes, sir."

Dimitri was not only the doctor's assistant, he was his bodyguard, as well. In fact, Dimitri would do almost anything the doctor asked of him. That was one of the reasons Dr. Cecil had brought the big man with him to America when he left England.

Their flight from England was a hasty one. The law had begun to close in on them, and to be taken would have interfered with Henry Cecil's work. Their only option was to leave the country, and Cecil chose to leave the continent, as well. In the dead of night they boarded a freighter that was heading for America, and they paid a pretty penny for the passage.

Upon their arrival in New York Harbor Cecil quickly decided they would not stay there. No, that was still too close to England. He chose to take them to the midwest, largely because he thought the West would be filled with savages. Dimitri was an able bodyguard, but he did not know how the man would fare against godless savages.

When they came to Cleveland Cecil knew he had found the right place. A large city, but not so large that it would have a decent metropolitan police department. Also, not so small that their experiments would be immediately evident.

Cleveland seemed ideal. It had many cemeteries, and many men who were willing to work in them. Tonight they were meeting one such man, and when Cecil met with these creatures he always made sure that Dimitri was armed.

"Bring the buggy around, Dimitri."

"Yes, Doctor."

Ostensibly, Cecil ran a clinic. That's what it said on the front. But it was actually his laboratory, because he took no patients at this clinic. He had no time to work on the living. Not when there was so much work to be done with the dead.

Dimitri came around with the buggy and Cecil walked to it and got inside the covered part. He knocked on the sides then to let Dimitri know it was time to go. He knew which cemetery they were going to. During the course of the past six months they had been to several, but they had discussed earlier that night which one they would be going to when it was late enough.

It was to be a moonless night, and that was good. When Henry Cecil was wandering around cemeteries, dealing with the dregs of humanity who made their livings there, he preferred not to see them well, and not to be seen well. It was enough that they saw the hulking figure of Dimitri, and that they were able to feel the money that was pressed into their filthy hands.

And then there was the smell . . .

EIGHT

When Clint got back to his room he fitted the key into the lock, opened the door, and stopped. Unless the maids in the hotel had started wearing expensive perfume, someone either had been or was in the room. Clint knew of a killer once who wore women's perfume—the expensive kind—when he sneaked into a room to await one of his victims. When the man arrived and smelled the perfume he assumed he had a lady visitor, and was caught off guard. That killer had been dead a long time now, but the trick stayed in Clint's mind. He took the Colt New Line from his belt and entered the room.

The first room was empty, so that left the bedroom. He advanced carefully toward the door, gun held out in front of him. When he saw the form in his bed he relaxed. She was under the sheet, and the way it molded itself to her opulent curves made it obvious she was naked.

When she heard him in the door she started and turned, catching her breath for a moment.

"Sorry to startle you," he said. "I didn't expect you."

"You didn't?"

"No."

"I told you I wanted to see one of these rooms."

"I didn't think you meant tonight."

29

She sat up, holding the sheet to her breasts, bringing her knees up so she could encircle them with her arms. "I was right about the rooms. Much better than the ones at the Roberts."

"Maybe the mayor would move you here, if you asked him very nicely."

She made a face and said, "I know what he'd want in return. Anyway, the Roberts is closer to the theater. Are you coming to bed?"

"What about all that business about your beauty sleep and shadows beneath your eyes?" he asked.

"Oh, that," she said. "Actually, I need very little sleep. A few hours' nap and I'm fine. *Are* you coming to bed?"

"I thought I might—"

"You won't need the gun, then."

He'd forgotten it.

"Oh, right." He walked to the dresser and placed the gun on top, then began to remove his clothes.

"Do you always carry a gun?"

"Yes."

"Everywhere?"

"Yes."

"To dinner?"

"Yes."

"The theater?"

"Yes."

She hesitated, then asked "To bed?"

He inclined his head toward the bedpost, where his holster was hanging. "One is always close at hand."

She turned her head and said, "I can see that. How many times has somebody burst into your room intending to kill you?"

He dropped his underwear and said, "Too many to count. Do you want to leave?"

"Hmm?" she replied, staring at his crotch.

"I said do you want—"

"What I want," she said, "is for you to come over here

where I can see you. Here, on my side of the bed."

Obediently, he walked to her side, where she could see him better with light from the lamp on the table next to the bed.

"Oh my," she said, reaching out and fondling him, "very pretty, *very* pretty."

She stroked his shaft, which had still not fully extended, sliding her fingertips along the sensitive underside. He groaned and it swelled some more. She slid her hands down his outer thighs, then back up his inner thighs until she was fondling his heavy testicles.

"Very impressive," she said.

"What did you expect?"

"Truthfully? I expected one thing when you were just this attractive man across the room," she said, "but something else entirely when I found out who you were."

"And how do I stack up?"

"Mmm," she said, leaned over and put her mouth on him . . .

Later, while she was sitting astride him, he took great pleasure in looking up at her, taking her in while her eyes were closed and her head was thrown back. They were both sweating, and her full breasts were shiny with it, which gave her the look of a marble statue. Her nipples were hard and distended, and when he took her breasts in his hands and brought them to his mouth so he could nibble them she gasped and bit her lips, but continued to ride him up and down with a slow, dreamy cadence.

He reached for her hips at one point, then slid his hands beneath her butt, which was full and firm. Then he slid his hands up her back and pulled her down to him so he could kiss her. Her mouth was full and sweet, her tongue avid and alive in his mouth. She kissed him deeply, as if she were drinking from him, or wanted to smother him, but he matched her passion and her eagerness. He felt her begin to tremble as she neared her release and he took it upon

himself to increase their tempo, trying to time his own release to hers, but in the end, instead of going over the edge
together, he was just a few seconds behind her, tumbling,
emptying, ejaculating with dizzying intensity . . .

"You must think I'm terrible," she said later.

"No," he said, "in fact, I think you're wonderful."

"Forward, then," she said. "You must think me terribly
forward to come to your room like this."

"No," he said, "actually, I like a woman who knows what
she wants and is not afraid to reach out and get it."

"Well, that's me," she said, reaching out to stroke him
while they lay side by side on their backs. He felt his body
begin to react to her touch.

"I've always been able to reach out for what I want."

"Do you always get it?" he asked.

She hesitated, then said, "Not always, but close."

"And what do you want now?"

"Truthfully?" she asked. "I'm tired, I want to sleep."

"That sounds good to me," he said.

She tightened her hand on him and added, "But not all
night. Remember, I told you I only need a few hours."

"We have plenty of time to sleep," he said, "a few
hours . . . or maybe even more . . ."

"Oh no," she said, rolling toward him, "not more. That
would be a terrible waste of time."

She put her lips to his shoulder, then her tongue, tasting
his sweat. In her hand he swelled again to full readiness.

"Again?" she asked. "Already?"

"It's your hand touching me," he said. "Your mouth,
your tongue . . . what do you expect?"

"I expect to get a few hours sleep," she said, sliding
down his body, "later . . ."

As her mouth engulfed him he said, "Much later . . ."

NINE

When Dimitri stopped the buggy in front of his house Dr. Henry Cecil opened the door and stepped out.

"Take the buggy back, Dimitri, and then you can go home."

"Yes, sir. Uh, Doctor?"

"Yes, what is it?"

"About tomorrow night?"

"Tomorrow night?"

"Yes, sir . . . the opening?"

"Oh . . . oh, the play." Dimitri had seen this actress, Grace Abbott, when she performed at the Lyceum Theater in London, and she was opening a new play in town tomorrow night. The big man wanted desperately to go and see.

"What play is she doing?"

"*Macbeth*," Dimitri said. "I have seen her do it before. She is quite brilliant."

"Yes, yes, well, all right. You can have the evening off to go to your play."

"Thank you, sir. Would you like me to walk you to the door?"

"No, thank you," Cecil said, "I'm quite capable of walking myself to the door. Good night, Dimitri."

"Good night, sir."

"Bright and early Monday morning, don't forget."

"I won't, sir."

Dimitri drove the buggy away and Cecil walked to the front door of his house, unlocked the door, and entered. He'd chosen the house in Cleveland Heights because, in this affluent neighborhood, the homes were not very close to each other, and he valued his privacy above everything else.

He entered the house and immediately spotted Elvira's wrap, which meant she was still in the house. She had spent the night there, but he had not anticipated that she would still be there when he got home. It was good, though, that she was, because visiting the cemeteries excited him. Dealing with the people he dealt with did not. In fact, he thought he could still smell the man on him, but having their dealings in a cemetery more than made up for it.

And then there was his other problem, one of recent development. It seemed he was only able to perform sexually with Elvira. His first few times with her had been very exciting. He had picked her up in a less than desirable part of town and had paid her to come home with him. She'd been very surprised first that he would actually take her to his home, and second, that he lived in Cleveland Heights.

After they had been together a couple of times he had gone out and picked up another woman, blonde and busty, the direct antithesis of Elvira, and he had not been able to perform. Naturally, she had found this funny, so she ended up as one of his earlier "fresh" subjects.

The next time he had the urge he went out and found Elvira, and once again it was magical. After that he only did it with her.

And after that, she didn't charge him anymore. Oh, he gave her money, but now he gave her enough to keep her from having to "work" anymore. However, this was the first time she had remained in the house all day. He knew she hadn't left and come back, because he had not given her a key, and she did not know where one was.

He started to undress on the way up the stairs.

She heard him start up the stairs, and hurriedly went to the bed. She was naked, and ran her hands over her long, slender body. Her breasts were little more than handfuls, her nipples pale pink, her skin alabaster. She tweaked her nipples to get them hard. She knew this excited him, to think that *she* was already excited by him.

He was going to think that she had been in his house all day. Little did he know that she had a key, one that had been made for her by her man, Spender. The first time Cecil had ever taken her to his house she'd gone home and immediately told Spender about him. It was Spender's idea to get Cecil addicted to her. In fact, she was getting him so addicted that he'd give her money any time she wanted now. Spender had a plan, though, and all she had to do was keep playing the good doctor along until her man—her *real* man—was ready to put his plan into effect.

She heard him coming down the hall so she reclined on her back and slid her hand down between her legs to get herself wet for him. Her eyes went to the closet where he kept his toys. The welts from the last time were almost gone, so she knew he'd want to play tonight.

She and Spender were going to get rich off this foreign doctor—if he didn't kill her first.

TEN

When Clint went to work the next morning he had that pleasant fatigued yet relaxed feeling one had after an eventful night with a beautiful woman. He looked at Grace, who had flipped over onto her stomach during the night and was still sound asleep. Her full breasts were crushed beneath her and he wondered how a woman as well endowed as she was could sleep comfortably that way.

He looked at the light streaming in through the window and surmised that it was later than he normally would have risen. He thought about waking her for more sex and then remembered that he was supposed to have breakfast with George Karl. They hadn't set a time, but he decided he'd better get up and get going.

The sheet had slid down to her thighs, leaving her majestic butt gloriously bare. He put his hand on one cheek and shook her gently, but she didn't stir. He leaned over and ran his tongue along the cleft between her cheeks, then bit her gently until she moaned and woke.

"Oooh," she said, "what a nice way to wake up." She rolled over onto her back and reached for him. "Come here, you beautiful man."

"Can't," he said, backing away. "I'm supposed to meet George for breakfast, and I'm starving."

"Well, so am I," she said. "You really help a girl work up an appetite. You're not going without me."

"That's not a problem with me if it isn't with you," he said. "Do you care what George thinks?"

"Not one bit. I need to freshen up, though, and I only have the same dress I wore last night."

The hotel had all the amenities—as the clerk had promised—including modern plumbing. There would be no washing with water from a pitcher and bowl.

"Why don't you get dressed and go down," she suggested, "and I'll join you when I get decent."

He couldn't resist. He said, "You look pretty decent to me right now," and kissed her. They pressed their naked bodies together and each started to respond until she pushed him away.

"No, no," she said, "you have to get ready."

"All right," he said, standing up. "Would you like me to order for you?"

"No," she said, "I'll order when I come down. You just meet your friend and start having your breakfast."

He washed and dressed hurriedly, then kissed her again before leaving the room and going downstairs.

Although they had not set a time, as Clint reached the lobby George Karl appeared through the front door. He saw Clint and walked to him, hand extended.

"Good timing," he said, as they shook. "Come on, I'll take you someplace special."

"Maybe another day," Clint said.

"Why?"

"We'll be three for breakfast."

"You dog," Karl said. "Already? That's another thing I remember about you, you attract them like flies. That hasn't changed after all these years?"

"I don't know if I attract them like flies," Clint said, "but I do all right." He wondered how Karl would react when he found out it was Grace Abbott.

"All right then," Karl said, "let's go into the dining room and get a table for three."

"After you," Clint said.

When Henry Cecil awoke he looked down at Elvira, lying next to him. The fresh welts on her pale ass were angry red. He'd put some special cream on them the night before, after they finished. He wondered if he might one day become so excited by what they did that he'd forget to stop. It had happened once before, in England, and he'd made sure it never happened again, but he also remembered the thrill he'd felt waking up next to a dead woman, knowing that he'd killed her sometime during the night, but not knowing exactly when. Had she been dead the last time he had sex with her? Had he been doing it with a corpse?

He was in a totally different country now. One mistake was permissible, wasn't it?

He put his hand on her back and stroked her. She was much too valuable to him now for that to happen, but maybe down the road, in the not-too-distant future.

When he was tired of her.

Both Clint and Karl ordered steak and egg breakfasts, and started on their coffee.

"Have you made up your mind?" Karl asked.

"George—"

"Before you tell me," Karl said, holding up his hands, "I want you to know I won't hold it against you if you decide not to stay. It was probably underhanded of me to ask you to come—"

"No," Clint said, "it would have been underhanded of you to ask me to come and also remind me in the telegram that I owed you."

"Well, yes," Karl said, "that would have been underhanded. But I want you to know—"

"George," Clint said, "before you go any further I've decided to stay and help as much as I can."

"That's great!" Karl said happily. "That's wonderful. I'll get the paperwork done today. I'll send a man for you a couple of hours after I leave. Everything should be ready by then."

"I'll carry your badge, just so I have official status," Clint said, "but I won't wear it."

"That's fine."

"And the mayor and Cleveland will pay for everything while I'm here?"

"Everything," Karl said.

"Good," Clint said, "because I'm going to need some clothes."

"That's fine. I'll send you to a good tailor I know."

"Good," Clint said. "Now, while we're waiting for our food, why don't you tell me what you know about this killer?"

ELEVEN

"First bodies started disappearing from graveyards," Commissioner Karl told Clint.

"And the families complained?"

"That's just it," Karl said. "There were no families. These were the bodies of homeless people being taken from unmarked graves."

"So who noticed and who complained?"

"There was this homeless man that everybody seemed to like. Hell, it was like they adopted him. They gave him clothes and food. About the only thing they didn't do was take him in."

"And what happened?"

"He finally died one night, and he was buried in an unmarked grave—but people would go to visit him. One of them found an empty hole one day, and made a report to us about it."

"Then what?"

"Then we checked out some other graveyards and found some more empty holes," Karl said. "Somebody had been stealing bodies."

"Why would anyone want dead bodies?" Clint asked. "Especially ones that have been in the ground for a while?"

41

"I don't know," Karl said, "but that wasn't the worst of it."

"I'm all ears."

"Eventually people started getting killed."

"This is the killer you've been talking about?"

"That's right," Karl said. "He started killing homeless people, only we didn't find them right away. Apparently he killed them, took them with him, and did God knows what with them, and then disposed of them. We'd find them days, sometimes weeks later."

"What's he been doing to them?"

"Our doctors can't tell."

"And you think this is the same person who was stealing the bodies from the ground?"

"At first look, no," Karl said. "We have every indication that different people have been involved."

"So you have more than one killer."

"Clint," Karl said, "I think that physically we have more than one killer, but I think they're being directed by one mind."

"And what's your proof of that?"

Karl sat back and said, "I don't have proof, I just have what I feel in my gut. There's one man behind this."

"When did it all start?"

"We can trace it back eight months."

"So either somebody went crazy eight months ago," Clint said, "or somebody new came to town."

"That's what I was thinking," Karl said. "Now people are worried the killer will start taking anybody, like their kids, and not just the homeless."

"Why are they thinking that?"

"We found a dead working girl one night," Karl said. "I think the guy took her home and ended up killing her, used her for whatever he's using them for, and then discarded her."

"You think he's using them for . . . what? Sex?"

"No," Karl said, "there's only been one woman, the prostitute."

"Some kind of experiments, then? Medical, maybe?"

"Why can't our doctors find anything?"

"Maybe you need a specialist."

"In what?"

"Good point."

The waiter came with their breakfasts and they sat back so he could serve them. When he left they leaned forward and picked up their utensils.

"So that's it," Karl said. "That's what I'm up against."

"I don't know what I can do for you, George."

"Maybe I just need someone with a new outlook," Karl said, "somebody I can trust, somebody who'll come up with new ideas or new observations."

"I'll do what I can."

"After you come to headquarters and we do the paperwork the mayor will want to talk to you."

"Why?"

"He likes to interview his new city employees."

"He told you to give me anything I want, right?"

"Right."

"Well, I don't want to be his employee," Clint said. "I want to be yours."

"You *will* report to me."

"And only you," Clint said. "I don't want him to have any authority over me."

"I don't think he'll go for that," Karl said, "unless you give him something in return."

"Like my name in the paper?"

"Yeah, like that."

Clint thought a moment, then said, "To hell with it. I tell you what. He can use the Gunsmith name, but not mine."

"I'm not sure I know the difference."

"That's okay," Clint said. "I do."

"Okay," Karl said, "I think that'll do it for him."

"Fine," Clint said. "I'll want to buy my new clothes before I meet with him."

"Okay."

"And I want to attend the first performance of Grace's play tonight."

"Fine."

"And here's our other guest for breakfast," Clint said, as Grace Abbott came into the dining room.

Without looking Karl signalled the waiter to come over.

"Escort the lady to our table," he said.

"Yes, sir."

The waiter went to the door, exchanged a few words with Grace, and started leading her to their table. Unable to control his curiosity Karl finally turned to take a look. He recognized Grace Abbott, looked quickly at Clint, and then said, "You *dog!*"

TWELVE

"Miss Abbott," Karl said, standing. Clint also stood.

"Commissioner."

The waiter held her chair and she sat down. Clint didn't know how she did it but she looked fresh as could be and, somehow, she had found something else to wear. It was a simple cotton dress, but on her it looked special.

"May I get you something, madame?" the waiter asked.

She looked at what Clint and Karl were having and said, "Yes, I'll have the same thing the gentlemen are having."

"Very good. I'll bring it right out."

As the waiter left Grace grabbed Clint's cup and began to drink his coffee.

"Are you two discussing business?"

"We were, yes," Karl said.

"Has Clint agreed to help you catch your killer, Commissioner?" she asked. "Or is he making you wait for your answer."

"Well, actually—"

"Because I think he should stay in Cleveland and help you," she said, without giving Karl a chance to answer. "After all, what are friends for, right?"

"Well, right—"

"So what do you say you give him your answer, Clint?"

she said. "And then maybe we can go on and talk about something more pleasant . . . like which of my performances you gentlemen are going to come to."

"Miss Abbott—" Karl said, but a look from Clint cut him off.

"Okay, Grace," Clint said, "I'll take your advice. George, I'll stay and help you."

"You . . . will?" Karl asked, slightly confused.

"Yes, I will," Clint said, trying to send the man signals with his eyes. "Why don't you send a man to pick me up in a couple of hours. I'll come to your office and we can finalize things there."

Karl finally realized that Clint wanted Grace to think that she had convinced him to stay.

"All right, Clint," Karl said. "That's what we'll do."

"There, are you happy now?" Clint asked Grace.

"Very."

"Do you roll right over men this way back East, too?"

"Oh no," she said to Clint, "back East they're much easier."

Karl was the first to finish his breakfast and then he excused himself.

"I do have some paperwork to get to," he said, standing up. "Clint? A couple of hours in my office?"

"I'll be there, George."

"Miss Abbott, I hope to see you perform tonight."

"I'll look forward to seeing you in the audience, Commissioner."

As Karl walked away from the table Grace said to Clint, "You're a lousy liar, did you know that?"

"When did I lie?"

"You'd already given him your answer before I came down."

"Yes, I did."

"Why did you let me believe I talked you into it?"

"Because you wanted to. When did you figure it out?"

"During the course of the conversation. A few things were said that made it clear. Now he thinks that the two of you fooled me."

Clint laughed. "I'll tell him we didn't fool you at all. I'll tell him you're too smart for a couple of old westerners to fool."

"Good," she said, "you tell him that."

Clint pushed his plate away with nothing left but bone. Grace also pushed hers away. It was three-quarters empty, but it was a pretty impressive display of eating for a woman, and he said so.

"Oh, that was one thing I could always do was eat," she said. "You'd be surprised at some of the things I've done to eat."

"Like what?"

"Well like . . . everything short of prostitution."

"What's short of prostitution?"

"Well, when I was younger I wanted to be on stage so bad that I took my clothes off."

"On stage?"

"That's right," she said. "Men applauded, and then fed me. Back then that was all I wanted."

"Well, at least you're not ashamed of it."

"Oh, not at all," she said. "I told you, I've done everything but work as a whore. I'm not ashamed of any of it." She dropped her napkin in her plate. "I have to get back to my hotel. Put me in a cab again?"

"Will you stay in it, this time?"

"I swear," she said, raising her right hand.

They stood up and left the dining room together. He walked her to the front door and asked the doorman to get her a cab to the Roberts Hotel.

"How did you do it?" he asked her.

"Do what?"

"Manage to look so wonderful this morning . . . and where did you manage to get a new dress?"

She smiled and said, "A girl's got to have some secrets, Clint."

"Your cab, ma'am," the doorman said.

She kissed Clint's cheek and said, "You better come tonight."

"I'll be there."

"I'll leave tickets for you for every performance," she said. "Front row, so you can't tell me you were there when you weren't."

"That would be lying," he said. "I would never lie to you."

She smiled, touched his face, and said, "That alone would make you a very special man."

He watched as the doorman walked her to the cab, and realized the man was enjoying the view from behind. He helped her into it and as it drove away the doorman saw that Clint had been watching him. The man returned with a sheepish look on his face.

"Sir, I'm sorry—"

"Forget it," Clint said. "I'd worry about you if you weren't watching her."

THIRTEEN

Two hours later Clint was waiting in the lobby when the same officer who picked him up at the train station the day before entered the lobby looking for him.

"Mr. Adams," Officer Hedges said. "Commissioner Karl sent me to take you to headquarters."

"Hedges," Clint said. "It's nice to see a familiar face."

They went outside and Clint saw that it was not a Cleveland police department buggy or cab that had been sent for him.

"The commissioner instructed me to take civilian transportation," Hedges said, as if reading Clint's mind.

"I see."

"Do you? Because I don't."

"Well, I suppose if the commissioner wanted you to know why he would have told you."

"Yes, sir."

They got in and Hedges told the civilian driver to take them to police headquarters.

When they got there they walked in together and approached the front desk. There was an older man with a worn uniform and sergeant's stripes standing behind the big front desk.

"Sergeant," Hedges said, "this man is here to see the commissioner."

"Does he have an appointment?"

"Yes."

The sergeant looked at Clint.

"Second floor," he said. "You can take the elevator or, if you hate the damned things like I do, the stairs."

Clint didn't exactly hate elevators, but he said, "I'll take the stairs."

"Good choice."

"Thanks for your help, Officer," he said to Hedges.

"I could take you up, if you like."

"No," Clint said, "I think I can find it."

"His office has his name on it."

"That'll help," Clint said.

"Don't you have something you should be doing, Hedges?" the sergeant asked.

"Yes, sir, I do—"

"Then get to it."

"Yes, sir."

"Thank you," Clint said to the sergeant.

"Good luck with those stairs," the man said.

Clint didn't know what to say to that so he took the stairs to the second floor and found himself in a white hallway with green walls and a black and white checkerboard floor. There were names and numbers on all the doors so he just kept walking until he came to one with a gold plaque that had POLICE COMMISSIONER GEORGE V. KARL inscribed on it.

He entered without knocking and a young girl peered up at him through glasses that magnified her eyes somewhat, giving her an owlish look.

"Can I help you?"

"I'm here to see the commissioner."

"And your name?"

"Clint Adams."

"Oh, of course, Mr. Adams. The commissioner is expecting you. Go right through that door."

"Thank you."

He went to the door behind her, opened it, and entered. George Karl was standing with his back to the door, hands clasped behind his back, looking out the window at the Cuyahoga River. When he heard the door open he turned and saw Clint.

"Well, thank God."

"Did you think I was going to change my mind, George?" Clint asked, closing the door behind him.

"I was hoping you wouldn't," Karl said. "Can I get you some coffee?"

"Sure, why not?"

"Have a seat."

Karl went to the door, opened it, and said, "Addy, get us some coffee, will you? Thanks, honey."

He closed the door and returned to his desk. He sat down, opened the top drawer, took out a brown envelope, and pushed it across to Clint.

"What's this?"

"Your bonafides," Karl said.

Clint took out a bunch of papers and a badge with the words CLEVELAND POLICE DEPARTMENT inscribed on it. The papers identified him as an employee of the police department.

"Did you talk to the mayor?"

"Yes," Karl said. "It went pretty much as we figured it would. You'll report to me, not to him."

"And the newspaper?"

"Tomorrow's *Plain Dealer* will announce that the Gunsmith has been hired by the police department in an advisory capacity."

"Well," Clint said. "That's something. I thought it would announce me as some sort of hired gun."

"Believe me," Karl said, "he would have loved to put it in that way, but I talked him out of it."

"Do I need to carry these?" Clint asked, brandishing the papers.

"No, as a matter of fact, you can leave them right here with me."

"But the badge?"

"I'd carry that, if I was you," Karl said. "That'll get you into places you couldn't get into up to now."

"So what's our first step going to be, George?"

"First," Karl said, "you're going to meet my two chiefs."

"Well," Clint said, "this should be interesting."

FOURTEEN

Both the chief of detectives and the chief of police had offices on the same floor. Before going to see them, however, Karl filled Clint in on their backgrounds. He did this while they drank the coffee Karl's secretary, Addy, brought for them.

"The chief of police is Harold Carter. Harry was in place when I got here. He's old line, and I couldn't have replaced him if I wanted to."

"Did you want to?"

"Yes."

"Why?"

"I think he's incompetent," Karl said. "Oh, I think he knew his job once, but now he's coasting."

"Why can't you get him out?"

"He's got a lot of political friends."

"Like the mayor?"

"Like the mayor."

"So is he in the way as far as this investigation goes?"

"No," Karl said, "he's pretty much staying out of it and leaving it to the chief of detectives."

"And who might that be?"

"Walt Coburn."

"I know that name," Clint said, frowning, then placing

it. "I thought he was with Wells, Fargo, working under Jim Hume."

"He was," Karl said. "I hired him away from there when I got this job. Biggest mistake I've made in this job, so far."

"I thought he was good."

"He's very good," Karl said, "but he's also ambitious."

"Ah," Clint said, "he's after your job."

"If he can find this killer and let it be known that he caught him I might have a problem holding onto this job."

"So we have to get to this killer before he does."

"Right."

"And that's why you don't know who to trust."

"Right again."

"Is there one detective under you that you can trust?"

"Yes," Karl said, "you'll be meeting him after I introduce you to the two chiefs."

"And what's his name?"

"It's Spender," Karl said, "Eddie Spender."

They walked down the hall to a door that had a similar plate to the one on Karl's door. This one read HAROLD CARTER, CHIEF OF POLICE George Karl opened the door without knocking. The woman sitting at the desk there was roughly three times the age as Karl's girl, Addy—or, at least, she looked it.

"Good morning, Commissioner," she said, almost snapping to attention.

"Good morning, Miss Hyatt," Karl said. "I'd like you to meet Clint Adams. He's going to be in the building for a while."

"In the building?"

"He'll be working here," Karl said, "reporting directly to me. You're to give him anything he wants. Understand?"

"Why, yes sir," the woman said, "if you say so."

"Is the chief in?"

"I'll have to check, sir."

"You do that, Miss Hyatt."

"I'll be right back."

She stood, turned, and went through a door Clint assumed led to the chief of police.

"She's been working for Harold since—well, for years. She's probably warning him that I'm here, which means she's either waking him, or giving him a chance to try to sober up."

Before Clint could say anything the door opened and Miss Hyatt's gray head appeared.

"The chief is in, Commissioner."

"Thank you, Miss Hyatt."

Both he and Clint walked past the woman into the chief's office, and she closed the door behind them.

The man behind the desk was tall and painfully thin, to the point of being gaunt. His uniform suit was rumpled, and his eyes seemed a bit bleary. Clint assumed that Karl had hit the mark with one of his guesses. The man looked like someone who had just awakened from a sound sleep.

"Commissioner," Harold Carter said. "What can I do for you this morning . . . sir?"

The "sir" sounded to Clint like an afterthought, and he guessed that this was the way the chief usually addressed George Karl.

"I'd like you to meet Clint Adams, Harold," Karl said. "He's a friend of mine who has agreed to come into the department as a special agent, reporting to me."

"Special agent?" Carter said, frowning. "He's the— you're the Gunsmith, right?"

"That's who he is," Karl said. "He's going to be helping me track our killer."

"Oh, I see," Carter said. "You felt the need to go outside the department for help, then?"

"I did."

"Without consulting me?"

"I wasn't aware that I had to consult you before making my decision, Harold," Karl said.

"Well . . . I was only speaking of common courtesy, Commissioner," Harold Carter said, backing off a bit. "Does, uh, Chief Coburn know about this?"

"He does not," Karl said. "We'll be going to his office next, though, to make introductions. So you see, Harold, I came to you first."

That seemed to do little to mollify the chief of police.

"I'll want you to give Clint every cooperation, Harold. Is that understood?"

Harold Carter stood at attention and said, "Oh yes, Commissioner, it's understood. Welcome to the department, Mr. Adams."

The timber of the man's voice did little to make Clint feel welcome.

"Thank you, Chief."

"Well," Karl said, "we'll see you later, Harold. After we talk with Walt I might decide to have a meeting."

"I'll be right here, Commissioner."

"Yes," Karl said, "I know."

He turned and led Clint out the door.

FIFTEEN

The meeting with chief of detectives Walt Coburn went a little differently. They entered his office without knocking. Coburn's girl was about the same age as Addy.

"Hello, Commissioner. He's in his office."

"Thanks, Betty."

They went to Coburn's door, knocked, and entered.

"Good morning, Commissioner," Coburn said, from his desk.

" 'Morning, Walt. Want you to meet a friend of mine."

Coburn stood up for the introduction, revealing himself to be under six feet, slender but healthy looking. He had quick, intelligent blue eyes, and an engaging smile. He was in long white shirtsleeves, his jacket hanging over the back of his chair.

"This is Clint Adams."

"Adams," Coburn said, extending his hand across his desk. "I know the name and the reputation. I've heard about you from Jim Hume."

The two men shook hands.

"What brings you to Cleveland?"

"He's here to help us."

Coburn looked puzzled.

"With what?"

"The murders."

Coburn was still smiling, but it was not as engaging as before.

"We have that under control, Commissioner," the chief of detectives said.

"No, Walt, we don't," Karl said. "We can use the help."

"No offense, Adams," Coburn said, "but the last time I looked you weren't a detective."

"That's what I told George," Clint said. "This isn't my idea, but it's not his either."

"Oh? Whose is it?"

"The mayor's," Karl said. "He heard that Clint was in town visiting me and he insisted I enlist his help."

"Ah, I see," Coburn said. "Well, we can't very well tell the mayor to mind his own business, can we?"

"No, we can't," Karl said.

"Well, I guess we can put him on the payroll, give him a badge, call him a detective, and have him stay out of the way. He could go to the theater, maybe—"

"No," Karl said, "if he's here and he's agreed to help, I'm going to use him."

"As what?"

"He'll be a special agent reporting to me."

"Special agent," Coburn said.

"See? Karl said. "We're not calling him a detective."

"I can see that. So he'll report to you?"

"That's right."

"Will I, at least, know what he's doing?"

"Every step of the way," Karl lied.

"And how does Chief Carter feel about this?"

"About the same way you do, Walt," Karl said. "He doesn't like it."

"I see."

"But neither one of you has to like it."

"I understand. Well, Adams," Coburn said, directing his attention to Clint, "if I can do anything to help you, just let me know."

"I'll try to work with you, Chief Coburn," Clint said. "I know your reputation as a detective is well deserved. Believe me, I'll try not to be in your way."

"I doubt you will be," Coburn said. "Commissioner, maybe we four should get together for a meeting sometime today?"

"Good idea, Walt," Karl said, "and I want Eddie Spender to be there, as well."

"Spender? Why?"

"He's a good man."

"Yes, he is, but so are a few of my other men."

"Fine," Karl said, "have them come to the meeting, as well. Why don't we set it up for three o'clock, in the meeting room down the hall."

"Three o'clock," Coburn said. "My men and I will be there, Commissioner."

"Fine," Karl said. "We'll see you later, then."

"Adams," Coburn said, extending his hand for another handshake. "It's good to meet you."

"You too, Chief."

"Call me Walt," Coburn said. "Maybe we can have dinner one night while you're here. We have some friends in common."

"Yes, we do," Clint said. "I'd like that."

"Good," Coburn said. "We'll do it."

"See you later, Walt," Karl said, and led the way out.

Out in the hall they started walking toward Karl's office. He exchanged greetings with several officers along the way.

"What do you think?" he asked Clint.

"Coburn is smooth," Clint said, "Carter less so."

"I agree. Walt is already trying to recruit you to his side."

"You don't have to worry about that, George," Clint said. "I'm your man while we're here."

"I know that," Karl said. "Let me get my hat from my office and we'll go over to city hall to see the mayor. We should be back in time for the three o'clock meeting."

"Fine."

They went into the office and Clint waited outside with Addy while Karl went to get his hat.

"Addy," he said, when he came out, "please let Chief Carter know that we'll be meeting in the room down the hall at three."

"He'll ask who's going to be there, sir," Addy said.

"Yes, he will," Karl said. "You tell him I'll be there, and I want him there. That's all he needs to know."

"Yes, sir," Addy said. "I'll be sure to give him the message."

"We'll be at city hall," he told her, "but we'll be back by three for the meeting, if anyone's looking of me."

He turned to Clint and said, "Come on. Let's get this one over with and then we can get to work."

SIXTEEN

City hall was half a block from police headquarters so they walked there, still discussing the two chiefs Clint had met.

"So how are we going to handle them?" Clint asked.

"We're not," Karl said, "I am. You don't have to worry about them."

"What about Coburn's invitation?"

"Have dinner with him," Karl said, "see what he has in mind. I don't care. All I'm saying is you don't have to report to either one of them—or the mayor."

"Does he understand what should go into the newspaper tomorrow?" Clint asked.

"He understands," Karl said. "Here we are."

City Hall was impressive. The lobby had marble floors and marble columns. They took a huge, winding staircase to the second floor, and Karl led the way to the mayor's office.

Inside they once again presented themselves to a secretary, but since Karl was not calling on a superior, they had to wait longer.

"He does this," Karl said to Clint, as they sat down to wait. "It's a show of power."

"I would have thought signing your paycheck was a show of power."

"That, too, but he has to play his little games."

Clint shook his head. "Politics."

"I know," Karl said, "but it's the arena I'm in now, Clint. I've got to play by their rules."

"Try making your own," Clint said. "You might make out better."

Before Karl could answer the mayor's secretary, a handsome, fortyish woman named Miss Dawson, said, "You can go in now, gentlemen. The mayor can give you five minutes."

"That's four more than I want," Karl said under his breath, and led the way.

"Ah, George, and Mr. Adams," the mayor greeted them. He was seated behind a huge cherry wood desk. "Excuse me if I don't get up. Please, have a seat. I have some fool meeting to go to in about five minutes, but I just wanted to welcome you to the team, Mr. Adams," he said, looking at Clint."

"Thank you, Mayor."

"The newspaper will carry the story tomorrow about you signing on as a special, uh, observer. Um, your special requests have been met. I don't anticipate that you will have any problem with the story."

"Fine."

"I want to thank you for agreeing to help us."

"I'll do what I can, Mayor."

"Have you met the chief of police and the chief of detectives?"

"I have."

"Good men, both of them," Morgan said. "Handpicked, one by me and one by George."

"I understand that."

Morgan looked at the clock and said, "Well, I'm afraid I have to go. Please feel free to call on me anytime, Mr. Adams. I'm at your disposal."

"Yes, sir," Clint said. "I appreciate that."

· They were almost to the door when the mayor called out, "Will I see you both at the theater tonight?"

Karl and Clint exchanged a glance, and then Karl said, "With any luck, yes sir."

"Excellent," Morgan said. "We must support the arts, you know."

"Yes, sir," Karl said, and ushered Clint out the door.

Walking back to police headquarters Karl said, "Thank God that's over with. We have plenty of time before our meeting. Let me show you where I do my drinking after work."

"But it's not after work yet," Clint said.

"That's okay," Karl said. "I could use a drink, anyway. Come on."

He crossed the street and headed away from police headquarters with Clint following closely. They walked several blocks and then ducked into a small saloon called Donnellys Tavern.

"Look out, boys," the bartender called out, "it's the police!"

There were only as few men in the place and none of them looked up. Karl led the way to the bar.

"Clint, this is Sean Donnelly. Sean, a good friend of mine, Clint Adams."

"Pleased to meet ya," Donnelly said. "What'll ya have, Commissioner?"

"Two beers," Karl said.

"Comin' up."

"This is where I come to get away from it all," Karl said.

Clint looked around. The place was small, intimate, well furnished. When Donnelly came back with the beers they were in frosty mugs.

"Coldest beer in Cleveland," Donnelly said.

It took only one sip for Clint to find out that Donnelly was most likely correct.

"Gonna sit at your table, Commissioner?" Donnelly asked.

"Not right now, Sean. We've got to get back for a meeting. I was just showing Clint the best place to go for a beer."

"Be seeing more of ya here, then?" Donnelly asked Clint.

"I'm sure you will."

Donnelly went to the other end of the bar and Clint asked, "Does anyone else come here?"

"The chiefs, you mean? No, there's another place closer to work that they go to. It's a club, really, full of businessmen and bankers. Not for me."

"The mayor?"

"He goes, too."

"But do you stop in there?"

"When I have to, but I prefer it here."

"Can't say I blame you. Can't fault the beer."

"Food's good, too," Karl said. "You'll have to try the Irish Stew."

"Sounds good."

They finished their beers and set the empty mugs on the bar.

"Let's get back for our meeting, then."

"Just what are we going to cover at this meeting?" Clint asked.

"I just want everybody to help you catch up," Karl said, waving to Donnelly and leading the way to the door. "Once you know what everbody else knows, maybe you'll come up with some ideas of your own."

Clint hoped he wouldn't disappoint his friend, who was counting on him to give more help than he might be capable of giving.

SEVENTEEN

Clint and Karl waited in the commissioner's office until three-oh-five and then walked down the hall to the meeting room. When they entered everyone else was already there. In attendance were Chiefs Carter and Coburn. Also, as requested by Karl, Detective Spender, along with Detectives Hamilton and Jordan, who were there at the behest of Chief Coburn. They were all sitting at a long wooden table, a couple of them drumming their fingers on it impatiently.

"Good, you're all here," Karl said. "For those of you who haven't met the newest addition to our apartment this is Clint Adams."

"*The* Clint Adams?" Eddie Spender asked. "The Gunsmith?"

"That's right," Karl said.

"He's a member of this department?" Warren Jordan asked. "Since when?"

"Since this morning," George Karl said. "He is a special agent reporting only to me."

"Working on what?" Detective Dan Hamilton asked.

"The homeless killer," Karl said, and then to Clint, "for want of a better name."

The three detectives all looked at their chief, Walt Coburn.

65

"Don't look at me that way," Coburn said. "This was the mayor's idea."

"But—and I mean no disrespect to Mr. Adams—" Eddie Spender said, "but he's not a detective."

"A point I made myself," Clint said.

"It doesn't matter," Karl said. "Mayor Morgan wants him on the payroll, and it's going to be in tomorrow's paper."

"Who's he going to be working with?" Hamilton asked. He and Jordan usually worked together.

"He's going to be with Detective Spender."

"Why me—uh, no disrespect intended," Spender said.

"None taken."

"He doesn't know the city," Karl said. "It's going to be your job to get him around."

"I'm his guide?" Spender asked.

"For want of a better name," Karl said, "you're his partner."

Spender didn't look happy, but he lapsed into silence.

"Okay," Karl said, "for the next half hour we're going to bring Clint up to date on what we've got on these killings."

"And the grave robberies," Hamilton said.

"Hamilton, you were the first one on those, so you start."

"Well," Hamilton said, "we got a report . . ."

For the next half hour each of the detectives took their turn filling Clint in on the investigation, so far. To Clint it sounded as if the policemen had all done whatever they could to find the killer. The fact was there were too many discrepancies in the crimes for any common denominator to be found, other than the fact that the victims were homeless and—for the most part—without families.

"And that's it," Walt Coburn said to Clint when Spender finished his report. "Now you know what we know."

"Doesn't seem like you left anything out," Clint said.

"We haven't," Coburn said. "We've tried everything. Any new ideas you might have will be welcome."

"I'll see what I can come up with."

"All right, that's it," Karl said. "Let's get back to work."

The men got up from the table and started for the door. The chief of police, Harold Carter, was the first one out. He had said nothing during the entire meeting. The others filed out behind him, with Spender and Coburn taking up the rear.

"Spender," Karl said.

"Yes, sir?"

"Don't leave the building," Karl said. "Clint will be joining you shortly."

"Yes, sir."

Detective Eddie Spender was shaking his head as he left the room.

"I can see what a welcome edition I am to this team," Clint commented when they were all gone.

"Don't worry about it," Karl said. "They'll all cooperate."

"Tell me why Coburn had Hamilton and Jordan in here."

"They're his boys," Karl said. "He recommended them when he took his job, and I hired them. They report to him, and I can't trust them as far as I can throw them."

"But you trust Spender?"

Karl hesitated, then said, "Within reason."

"Why?"

"Because I hired him *against* Walt Coburn's recommendation."

"So the fact that he's *not* Coburn's boy makes him the most trustworthy in your eyes."

"Right."

"But I shouldn't trust him too much."

"Right again."

"This is going to be a lot of fun," Clint said. "You know, from what I heard here today I can't see where there have been any holes in the investigation."

"Do you have any suggestions?"

"Not yet," Clint said, "but I would like to see a map of

the city with the sites of the grave robberies and the sites of the murders marked."

"Talk to Eddie," Karl said. "He had the same idea and put one together."

"Well, at least we're thinking alike there."

"Clint," Karl said, "I appreciate your help, but believe me, I don't expect any miracles. Maybe the mayor has the right idea. Maybe putting your name in the paper will scare the killer out of town."

"And how much do you believe that, George?"

Karl scowled and said, "Not much."

"No, I didn't think so." Clint stood up from the table. "Where do I find Spender?"

"Go up one flight, second door on the right is a room all the detectives use. You'll find him there. Good luck."

"Thanks," Clint said, starting for the door, "I'm really going to need it."

EIGHTEEN

Clint followed Karl's directions and found a room full of desks, with a detective at each one. It occurred to him that he'd forgotten to ask his friend where *he* would be working out of, but he decided that would be his hotel. There was no way he was going to fit into the picture he was looking at, at the moment.

As he entered the detectives looked up. Hamilton and Jordan looked away, but Spender waved him over.

"I guess you can share my desk," Spender said. "These others look empty, but they have men assigned."

"I don't think I'll be needing a desk," Clint said, "but thanks."

"What would you like to do first?" Spender asked.

"Well, I mentioned something to the commissioners about mapping out the sites of the crimes, but he said you'd already done that."

"Yeah, I thought it would be a good idea," Spender said. "I didn't get much support for it from these guys, but I set it up, anyway. It's in a room at the end of the hall. Come on, I'll show you."

Spender stood up and led Clint out of the room. He was about Clint's height and build, but ten or twelve years younger. He walked like a man who had spent most of his life in cities, and not much time on a horse.

"I don't know what kind of investigative techniques you've used in the past—" Spender started, but Clint stopped him.

"Whoa," he said, "investigative techniques? As you yourself pointed out, Detective Spender, I'm not a detective."

"Well," Spender said, looking sheepish, "I said that for the benefit of the others. I happen to know that you've solved your share of crimes around the country. I'm a student of crime, you see."

"Well," Clint said, "nothing I've ever done, or used, could be called a 'technique,' of any kind. Basically, I just do what comes logically."

"Logic," Spender said, "is the most important aspect of what I do. I can see we're already on the same track, here— even about this."

He gestured Clint into a room at the end of the hall—a room which, on the floor below, they'd had their meeting in. On the wall was a map of Cleveland and, as Clint got close, he could see that certain points on the map had been marked heavily with a pencil.

"The sites that are circled," Spender explained, "are the graves that were robbed. The sites enclosed in a square are where the murders took place—or where the bodies were found. We're not sure, in all cases, that the two are the same."

Clint moved closer to the map to study it.

"Where are we?" he asked.

"Here." Spender pointed. There were no marked sites anywhere near them.

Clint studied the map further, saw that certain areas were marked with names, like Shaker Heights, and Cleveland Heights and others.

"What do you have planned for tomorrow?" Clint asked.

"Nothing specific. Why?"

Clint turned away from the map to face the man.

"I'd like to visit each one of these sites."

"All of them?"

"If it's not a problem."

"It's not a problem for me. It might be time consuming, but it can be done."

"In one day?" Clint asked. "I won't need to spend very long at any one place."

"Sure, we can do it in one day," Spender said. "Why not? I got nothing better to do. I can take you to a good place to eat, too, when you get hungry."

"Look," Clint said, "I'm sorry as hell that you had to get saddled with me, but I'll try—"

"Hey, never mind," Spender said. "I only complained for the purpose of appearances. I'm really pleased that we'll be working together. See, I've read all about you."

"You can't believe everything you read."

"I know that," Spender said. "See, I'm really good at reading between the lines. Now I'll have a chance to see how right I've been."

"Well," Clint said, "I just didn't want you to think I'd be in the way."

"I don't," Spender said. "Those other guys, they're in the way. Neither Jordan or Hamilton knows a thing about logic. All they want to do is go stomping around and hope they run into the killer."

"What about Coburn?"

Spender turned and closed the door to the room, so they had more privacy.

"I read a lot about Coburn, when he was working for Hume over at Wells, Fargo. His reputation said he was a good detective, but I'm wondering how much of that was achieved by riding Hume's coattails. Do you know what I mean?"

"Yes, I do."

"He hasn't really shown me anything," Spender said, "and I know he opposed my hiring and that *he* recommended Hamilton and Jordan. None of that makes any points with me."

"I can see why it wouldn't. How do you feel about Karl. Had you read about him?"

"Him and you," Spender said. "Yeah, I read about Karl's day's as a railroad detective. He's about the only one I can talk to logically about all of this. He listens, and he lets me have my head. I like him."

"Good," Clint said, "then that's something else we agree on."

"It's getting a little late in the day," Spender said. "I usually go home about five, but I can hang around—"

"No, no," Clint said, "you go ahead. Got a wife waiting for you at home?"

"No, nothing like that," Spender said. "I just happen to have a life away from my job. Hey, do you want to get something to eat?"

"Not tonight," Clint said. "I'm supposed to go to the theater with the commissioner."

"Oh. Shakespeare," Spender said. "Really not my kind of theater, but I have seen that actress, Grace Abbott. *She's* my kind of theater."

"She's a beauty, all right."

"Okay, then," Spender said, "why don't we meet back here tomorrow morning at . . . nine?"

"Nine's fine."

"Good," Spender said. "I'll get a buggy from the department so we don't have to keep catching cabs, and we'll go and take a look at all the sites."

"Sounds good."

"Don't worry about stepping on my toes, Clint," Spender said. "If you come up with any fresh ideas, I'd like to hear them."

"I'm glad to hear that, Eddie," Clint said. "You don't know how glad I am to hear that."

NINETEEN

Clint stopped in to see Karl once more before leaving to go back to his hotel.

"How did it go with Spender?"

"Real well," Clint said. "Seems he's a student of crime and detection. He's read about you and me and who knows who else. Turns out he's real pleased I'm going to be working with him—or so he says."

"I wish I could trust him more," Karl said. "Eddie seems to be a really good detective."

"He and I are going to go out tomorrow and look at the crime sites," Clint said.

"His idea, or yours?"

"Mine," Clint said. "It's all I can think to do to get started."

"Sounds good to me. Say, you want me to swing by your hotel tonight, or should we meet at the theater?"

"Let's meet there," Clint said. "I'll just get in a cab and tell him to take me . . . where?"

"The Cleveland Center for the Arts."

"Wow. Fancy name."

"Fancy place," Karl said. "Wait until you see it."

"I'm looking forward to it."

They said their good-byes and Clint left the office. He

noticed that Addy's desk was empty, and figured she had probably gone home for the day.

Out front he found a cab, got in, and told the driver to take him to the Saxon Hotel.

Henry Cecil was sorry he had given Dimitri the night off to go to the theater. It wasn't that he had anything in particular for the man to do. There wouldn't even be another delivery until the next night. It was just that being at the clinic alone made him feel so . . . vulnerable. Sometimes he wished that he could transfer his brain into Dimitri's body. Nothing would be beyond him, then physically or mentally.

He wondered if there was a real way to accomplish that? Wouldn't that be a monumental scientific discovery?

Elvira waited for her man to come home from his day job. She didn't know why Eddie Spender insisted on remaining a police detective. It confused her that he seemed to live two lives, one during the day and one at night. She tried very hard to be the same person whether the sun was up or not. Spender seemed intent on remaining two different people, and to her that just sounded too damn hard.

She heard the door open downstairs and then his footsteps on the stairs as he came up. When the door opened she threw herself at him and shouted, "Baby!"

He kissed her soundly, cupping her ass with both hands and pulling her to him, then lifted her off her feet and walked her to the bed, which they tumbled onto together.

No real conversation would be exchanged for some time . . .

Dimitri dressed very carefully for his night at the theater. The love of his life, Grace Abbott, deserved the very best of him. He had first seen her perform in his native England, on the London stage, and she had taken his breath away that night. After that he dreamed about her, pined for her, followed her career as best as he could. When the day came that Dr. Cecil said they were leaving for America his heart leaped. He would be closer to his love, then, but never had he suspected that he would actually end up living in a city where she would come to perform.

This was beyond his wildest dreams, and he was bound and determined not to allow this opportunity to pass.

He would declare himself to her tonight!

Grace Abbott ran through her lines for the thousandth time, and wondered why it was she could remember Clint Adams' face better than she seemed able to remember her lines. She wondered if he would come to the performance tonight, hoped he would be in the front row, and hoped that she would not be so distracted if he was that she would flub her lines.

This was even worse than normal opening night jitters.

TWENTY

When Clint reached the theater he was surprised, despite the warnings from George Karl that the facility was modern. It was huge, with an ornate entryway that led to a high-ceilinged lobby that was filled with people. Luckily, Karl had been watching for Clint and came over as he entered.

"I'm impressed," Clint said.

"I told you that you would be. Come on, I picked up our tickets."

They wended their way through the crowd into the theater and made their way to their seats, which were in the front row. Slowly, the theater began to fill behind them.

"Where's the mayor?" Clint asked.

"He has a box."

Karl pointed and Clint looked up at the comical sight of the corpulent mayor sitting in his box.

"I'm glad I'm not sitting underneath it," Clint commented.

"You're right," Karl said. "I think I'm going to do something about losing some weight before I start to look like that."

They talked a little longer, but not about the case. Their small talk led to eventual silence, and then the curtain opened and the performance began. When Grace made her appearance she transcended the material for Clint, who was not a true theatergoer. While he recognized existence of the poetry in Shakespeare's words, he was much more of a Mark Twain man. For this reason he was free to enjoy not only Grace's performance, but her every move.

Which he did, avidly.

Grace was proud of herself. She had seen from backstage that Clint Adams was present. Once she knew that, she was able to compose herself, and suddenly all her lines came flowing back to her.

She performed flawlessly.

Dimitri was five rows back, seated in the center, and he was enthralled. Like Clint he followed Grace's every move, but unlike Clint he was totally unaware of the words she was speaking.

He became more and more obsessed with her as she moved about the stage, and by the end of the play was desperate to get to her, to talk to her.

As the applause died down and the theatergoers began to file out Dimitri started moving against the tide, trying to get to the front of the room instead of the back.

Trying to get to his love.

After the curtain closed Clint said, "I'm going to go backstage, George. Want to come?"

"Sure, why not?" Karl asked. "The mayor's going to be there, so why not me?"

They were able to move to stage left very easily, avoiding the crowds, and then slip backstage. They needed only to show their badges—Clint let the commissioner show his—to be admitted.

Backstage was a madhouse, with people moving in every direction, cast members hugging and kissing one another after the successful opening.

"Mr. Commissioner!" someone called.

Clint turned and saw a man in a black suit with frills on the chest and the cuffs of his white shirt coming toward them. He had long flowing hair that trailed behind him.

"What is that?" Clint asked.

"That," Karl said, "is the director."

"Mr. Commissioner," the man said, reaching them, "how utterly marvelous of you to come—and you brought a friend."

"David Manet," Karl said, pronouncing it like "magnet" but without the "g", "this is Clint Adams."

"Mr. Manet," Clint said, shaking the man's hand. "I enjoyed the play."

"I can only take credit for directing it," Manet said, holding his free hand to his chest while he continued to clasp Clint's in his other. "I cannot take credit for the immortal one's words."

"No," Clint said, retrieving his hand and wiping it dry on his trousers, "of course not."

"I know who you are, sit," the man said, to Clint.

"Do you?"

"Yes," Manet said, "you're the reason our Lady McBeth has been all aflutter all day. I hope you enjoyed her performance."

"I thought she was brilliant."

"Ravishingly brilliant, don't you agree?"

"I do, very much."

"Well, let me take you through this maze of humanity to her dressing room. Come along, come along . . . make way, darlings, make way!" he began to shout, waving his hands.

They followed in what was truly his wake.

When Clint entered the dressing room he saw Grace sitting in front of her dressing table, with her back to the mirror, accepting the congratulations of one dignitary or another.

"One of our local politicians and his wife," Karl said to Clint in a low voice.

The man was tall, handsome, and white haired and so was his wife.

Another couple stepped forward.

"A local businessman, who donates generously to the arts."

Clint wondered why supporters of the arts always seemed to be people who were . . . well, ugly. This man had all the appeal of a toad, and his wife looked ridiculous in a green dress that made her look as if she were walking around with a lily pad. Grace smiled and accepted their congratulations, smiling at them happily.

"Come, come," David Manet said to Clint. "I'll escort you to the front of the line, so that our diva knows you are here."

Once again they followed the little mini hurricane that Manet seemed to cause around him until they were facing Grace.

"What did you think?" Grace asked Clint, anxiously.

He took her hand, leaned over, and kissed it and said—so only she could hear it—"You were almost as brilliant tonight as you were last night."

She leaned forward, matched his tone, and said, "You are a bad man."

Clint stood up straight and gave her a more formal compliment on her performances, which she also accepted more formally.

He stepped aside to allow Karl to compliment her, and then suddenly the mayor was in the room—*filling* the room. It looked as if people were actually shoved out the door by his presence.

"My dear, you were wonderful, absolutely wonderful, wasn't she, gentlemen?" he asked, directing himself to Clint and Karl.

"She was indeed, Mr. Mayor," Karl said.

Mayor Morgan grabbed Grace's hand and began to slobber all over it. Clint had to give her credit, she managed to retrieve it gracefully and dry it somewhere without being obvious.

"Thank you, Mr. Mayor. I appreciate it."

"No, my dear," the mayor said, "Cleveland appreciates it."

He was about to say more when suddenly he was interrupted. They all turned their heads toward the dressing room door, because there seemed to be some sort of commotion going on outside.

TWENTY-ONE

Clint and Karl went out into the hall together. They saw a big man being held by two uniformed policemen—that is, they were trying to hold him, but they weren't having much success. As Clint watched, the big man swung one arm, bouncing one policeman off a wall, then the other arm, bouncing the other man off the opposite wall. Both men went down and the big man started down the hall toward them—and Grace's dressing room.

"I am here to see Grace Abbott," the man shouted. "Grace! My love!"

"He's nuts," Karl said to Clint. "We need more men."

"We could shoot him."

"No! That would look bad."

"Just in the knee."

"Clint!"

"All right, then, let's try to stop him."

As he approached them Clint and Karl spread out slightly.

"Is that her dressing room?" the man asked. He was well dressed, at least six four or five, maybe more, and he had an accent that sounded English to Clint, who had been to London once.

"Sir," Karl started, "I'll have to ask you to—"

"Get out of my way!"

He tried to go over Clint and Karl but it was Karl's bulk more than anything else that stopped him.

The people in the dressing room cowered to the sides, opening a path from the doorway to Grace, who was watching with wide eyes. The mayor, for all his size, had somehow done a disappearing act.

"Grace!" the man said, spying her sitting at her dressing table. "It's me, Grace!"

"Come on, friend," Clint said. He grabbed ahold of the man's left arm and it felt like a tree trunk. "You're making a scene, here."

"Let's get him out of here," Karl said, grabbing the other arm.

They squeezed him between them, so he didn't have the room to swing them around like he'd done the other two men. Behind him Clint saw the two men getting to their feet. He also saw Officer Hedges coming down the hall toward them. He approached the man from behind, swung something that impacted on the back of the big man's head. He grunted, but didn't go down. Hedges hit him again. This time the man's eyes rolled back and he slumped between Clint and Karl, who could not hold him up.

By this time the other two officers had joined them. Commissioner Karl told the three of them, "Get him out of here and throw him into a cell. He must be drunk."

"Yes, sir," Hedges said. He and the other two officers lifted the man up and dragged him back down the hallway and outside.

Clint went into the dressing room to Grace's side.

"Are you all right?"

"I'm fine," she said. "Did they . . . kill him?"

"No, just knocked him out. They'll let him sleep it off in a jail cell for the night," he said, even though he had smelled no liquor on the man.

"Miss Abbott," Karl said, "did you know him?"

"What? No, of course not."

"He seemed to know you."

"I have no idea who he was."

"He called you 'my love,' and called you by name."

"Commissioner," David Manet said, coming away from the wall he'd plastered himself to when the commotion began, "everybody knows her name, and most men love her. This man was obviously just an obsessed admirer."

"Has this happened to you before?" Karl asked her.

"I'm afraid so," she said, "but never anyone so ... so forceful, so ... big. For a moment there I didn't think you'd be able to stop him. I thought he was going to ... get me."

"There, there, sweeties," Manet said, taking her hand and rubbing it, "nobody's going to get you. Not as long as Mr. Adams is around ... isn't that right?"

"That's right," Clint said.

"Commissioner," Manet said, "I think Miss Abbott needs protection while she's in your city, and I think Mr. Adams is the man for the job."

"I understand the mayor already offered Miss Abbott a bodyguard, Mr. Manet," Karl said. "If she wants one I'd be glad to supply Officer Hedges for the job. Mr. Adams will be handling more ... pressing matters."

"Hedges?" Manet asked.

"The young officer who just knocked that man out and dragged him out of here." He made it sound like Hedges had done the whole thing himself.

"Well ..." Manet said, and looked at Grace Abbott. "What do you think, my sweet?"

"I don't need a bodyguard, David, thank you," she said. She looked at Karl. "Thank you, Commissioner, but no. I don't think this incident will be repeated."

"Well," Karl said, "if at any time you change your mind you only have to say so. All right?"

"Yes, thank you," she said. She looked at Manet now. "I think I'd like to get dressed now, David."

"We're still having our celebration dinner," he said.

"Yes, of course."

Manet looked at Clint and Karl.

"Both of you gentlemen will join us, I hope?"

Grace looked at Clint with pleading eyes—much as she had done the day before in the dining room of the Saxon Hotel. This time it didn't take him so long to read the message there.

"Of course," Clint said. "I'd be happy to."

"I have to get home," Karl said. "I have a wife waiting for me."

Clint looked at him, wondering if he was telling the truth. Up to this point nothing had been said about a wife. That would just be one more reason Karl would be desperate to keep his job.

"Very well, then," Manet said. "Come on, everyone out . . . out!" He looked at Clint. "Will you come outside and wait with me?"

"All right."

"Sweetie," the director said to Grace, "we'll be right outside, whenever you're ready."

"All right, David," she said. "Thank you."

And her eyes said "thank you" to Clint.

TWENTY-TWO

Clint had not expected to see Grace Abbott that night after the performance. He ended up going to dinner with Grace, David Manet, and members of the cast to celebrate their successful opening night. They went to a fairly fancy restaurant and he ended up sitting between one of the actors and a young woman who said she was an "understudy." He made the mistake of asking her to explain that and she then went on for the better part of an hour, never using one word where five or six would do. Every so often he would steal a glance down the end of the table at Grace, who was looking back at him almost every time while David Manet sat to her left, held her hand, and spoke into her ear. Clint began to think that there was more than a director/actress relationship going on there. He wondered if he had stepped into the middle of something.

Halfway through dinner it became apparent to him that the "understudy" was expecting to go back to his hotel with him. He hadn't entertained the thought at all—although she *was* young and *very* pretty—until she started talking about Grace and David Manet.

"You wouldn't know it to look at him," she said, "but our director is a real ladies' man."

"Is that right?"

"They say he sleeps with all his leading ladies."

Clint looked at her and said, "And not with the under-studies?"

"Oh," the girl said, "never with the understudies—unless they step into the leading roll, of course."

"And that only happens when the leading lady is unable to perform?"

"That's right."

"Then you have a chance."

"Well," she said, "first, I'm not the leading lady's un-derstudy, and second, David is not my type." She touched his arm. "You are."

"I'm very flattered."

"I like rugged, western-looking men."

It had also become clear to him during the dinner that, although the girl—whose name escaped him throughout the meal—was attracted to him, she had no idea who he was.

"You watch," she said. "When we leave here David and Grace will get into the same cab together and go back to their hotel."

"Which hotel is that?"

"The Roberts."

"Is that where everyone is staying?"

"Oh no," she said, "the cast is scattered about in differ-ent, much smaller hotels. Nothing so nice as the Roberts."

"And David and Miss Abbott," he said, "they're sharing a room?"

"Well," she said, "not technically. I mean, they each have their own room, but . . . where are you staying?"

After dinner they all filed out the front door to the street and cabs began to arrive to take them to their hotel. The understudy—he didn't know whose understudy she was—was hanging on Clint's arm.

"Okay, watch," she said. "David and Grace will get into the first cab that arrives."

Just as she predicted a cab stopped, one that the director

had obviously ordered, because it was a handsome cab, unlike the ones that arrived after it. They said good-night to everyone—Grace catching Clint's eye once—got into it and drove away. After that cast members began sharing cabs according to what hotels they were staying at.

"Which hotel are you staying in?" Clint asked the girl.

"Well," she said, looking up at him with pretty blue eyes, "tonight I was hoping . . . yours?"

He looked at her pretty face, her pale skin and small, sexy mouth and said, "Why not?"

Dimitri sat in his cell, exhausted by his attempts to batter his way out with his body. It soon became evident to him that he would not be getting out until they were ready to let him out. From the comments of the officers who had thrown him in there, they thought he was drunk and expected him to "sleep it off."

He finally fell back onto the filthy cot and tossed one arm across his face. This was not the way this night was supposed to go, and somebody was going to have to pay.

TWENTY-THREE

Having sex with the understudy was very different from having sex with Grace Abbott.

Her name was Sherrill, and while Grace had been experienced and self-assured, knowing where to touch and when, Sherrill was more eager and inexperienced—but she was willing to learn.

And then there was the physical difference. Grace Abbott was opulent, with curves that created shadows and hallows on her body that could be explored. Sherrill was smaller, and taut. Her breasts were like small peaches, her hips very slender, her butt small and solid. There was not an ounce of fat on her.

Clint took her through the lobby and her eyes got big as she looked around. When they got to his room her eyes got big again as she oohed and ahed and looked around. Then he took her into the bedroom and she fell in love with the bed.

"It's so big!" she said, bouncing on it like a little girl. "The bed in my hotel room is small and . . . squishy. This is so firm."

After that Clint went to her and began to undress her. She moaned and sighed as he touched her, and then he undressed for her and her eyes got big again.

"Oh, my," she said, when he was naked, because he was fully erect. Being with a girl like Sherrill was exciting in a different way than being with a woman like Grace—but the effect was the same.

Clint got into bed with Sherrill and began touching her. He learned quickly that she was not greatly experienced, had not been with men who were very experienced or good at giving women pleasure. He decided to do his best to give her a night to remember, just in case it wasn't repeated.

He kissed her sweet mouth, caressed her body, kissed her neck, and her firm little tits, bit her nipples, licked them, kissed his way down over her taut belly until mouth and nose were nestled in a small patch of pubic hair. Her own hair was auburn, but down between her legs it was red and wispy. He delved into her with his tongue, feeling her body tense, then relax, and when he slid his hand beneath her to cup her firm little ass and lift her he was able to lick the length of her easily and she began to buck and spasm.

He slid onto her right away, holding his weight off her, then sliding himself inside. He moved slowly, at first, long, slow strokes that made her groan each time he was fully inside of her and then suddenly she was at it again, spasming and showing surprising strength, as if she was trying to buck him off and then he exploded inside of her and she bit his shoulder to keep from screaming.

"Oh wow," she said, a little later. "Oh, God. I've *never* felt anything like that before. I feel like I should . . . thank you, or something."

"You did," he said, touching the bite on his shoulder.

She touched it too and said, "Oh, gee, did I do that?"

"You were the only other one here."

"I'm so sorry," she said, and kissed it gently. "Do you think she'll be mad?"

"Who?"

"Grace. Do you think she'll be mad when she sees it?"

"What makes you think she's going to see it?"

"Oh, come on," she said, smiling, pressing up against him, pulling the sheet up over both of them. "I may be inexperienced—more inexperienced than I thought, actually—but I'm not stupid. I can see that you and she have slept together."

He hesitated, wondering if he should deny it, then said, "Was it that obvious?"

"Only to another woman," she said. "Not to a *man*. I mean, David had no idea, I'm sure."

"I didn't know about David."

"Oh, I'm sure you didn't," she said. She was rubbing her palm over his belly in circles, enjoying the way his skin felt against it. He was enjoying the way her palm felt doing it.

"So, I just want you to know that I don't expect to repeat tonight," she said.

"Sherrill—"

She moved her hand lower and said, "I mean, not another night. I do expect to repeat again tonight, though."

"Sherrill—"

Her hand was stroking him now, and he was swelling to her touch. Her hand was small, and she closed her fist around him and began rubbing him up and down.

"I'm not totally inexperienced, though," she said, ducking under the sheet, and she proceeded to show him . . .

George Karl couldn't sleep. He slipped out of bed so as not to wake his wife and went downstairs to his den. He hadn't told Clint Adams that he'd met someone when he moved to Cleveland—a widow who was ready to marry again—and that they'd bought a big house. He hadn't wanted any of that to factor into Clint's decision whether to stay and help or leave.

Now that Clint had decided to stay he was worried. What if he wasn't able to help? Was this his last chance, then?

How long would the mayor give them now before he expected results?

He hoped that Clint and Spender would be able to work together successfully. Maybe they'd complement each other, the way he and Clint had done so ten years ago, when he was working for the railroads.

Working for the railroads had been simpler, straightforward, very little politics involved. At first, when he took this job, he didn't think he'd be able to handle the politics, but then it became a game. Now, however, it was all a desperate game. He couldn't afford to lose this job, and this house, not with a wife that was used to both. Her first husband had been a minor politician, and she knew her way around. She was able to help him fit in, but her help would only take him so far.

"George?"

He turned his head. He'd been sitting at his desk, but had turned the chair around so that his back was to it, and the door. He hadn't heard her come in. He turned and looked at her now. She was a handsome woman in her forties, ten years younger than him. He wondered still, after being married for a couple of years, what she saw in him that made her want to become Mrs. George Karl.

"Can't you sleep?" she asked, coming to him and putting her arms around him from behind. He loved those arms, loved how they made him feel. This was his first marriage, and he had a lot to learn about living with a woman, and sharing.

"Not very well," he said, touching her hands. "I didn't want to wake you."

"I'm awake," she said. "How about a cup of tea?"

"You, too?" he asked.

"Yes."

"All right."

She kissed the top of his head and said, "I'll come and get you when it's ready."

"All right."

"I love you."

"I love you, too."

She turned and left, and he swiveled the chair around and stared at the door. Maybe, he thought, he just needed a simpler life.

Spender was careful not to touch the welts on Elvira's pale butt. He kissed her back, her shoulders, ran his hands up the backs of her thighs, then probed between them, beneath her, until his fingertips were wet.

All of her customers thought she liked it rough, but Spender was the only man who knew that the real woman responded to a gentle touch. Or maybe it was just that she responded to his gentle touch.

"Is he almost ready to be taken?" he asked, stroking her gently.

"Mmm, yes, baby. Almost ready."

"Good," he said, looking at her ass. "I hate when he marks you. He's going to pay and pay big."

She opened her mouth to answer, but he had slid one finger into her and she gasped and used her unusual muscle control to trap it there.

"He's gonna pay big," he said into her ear.

TWENTY-FOUR

"So?" Sherrill asked, in the morning, as they dressed for breakfast.

"So what?"

"Do you think she'll be mad?"

He leaned over and kissed her.

"After last night why would I care if she's mad?"

"So you want to see me again?"

"Sherrill—"

"See? I knew it. You want her." She shook her head. "Why am I always the understudy?"

"You're not."

"It's okay, really," she said. "I'm used to it."

"You're not an understudy," he said. "I do want to see you again. It's just that . . ." He trailed off.

"Just that what?"

"I'm going to be a little busy."

"Oh, that's right," she said. "You're working for the police."

"That's right."

"And you won't have time to see both of us."

"Sherrill—"

"Okay," she said, "I'm teasing. I'll stop. Do you have time for breakfast?"

"A quick one," he said. "I have to be someplace at nine sharp."

"It's eight," she said. "We better go."

She thoroughly enjoyed the indoor plumbing, but unlike Grace she did not have a problem wearing the same clothes. They went down to the dining room together for breakfast.

They were served by the same waiter who had served Clint, Karl, and Grace Abbott the morning before.

"Good morning, sir."

"Good morning."

"Will there be, uh, any others for breakfast?"

"No," Sherrill answered before Clint could, "just the two of us, and we're in a hurry."

"Very well, miss," he said. "What would you like?"

"Bring us whatever Mr. Adams had yesterday."

"Yes, miss."

"I hope you don't mind that I ordered," Sherrill said.

"I don't mind at all," he said.

"Some men mind."

"I happen to like what I had yesterday."

"Where are you from, originally?" he asked.

"Well," she said, putting her elbows on the table and crossing her arms, "that's always a good sign."

"What is?"

"When a man asks a question like that . . . isn't it?"

"A good sign of what?"

"That he's interested."

"I thought that would be obvious, by now."

"Look, Clint," she said, "I know I shanghaied you, last night. You never intended or expected to ask me to come back here with you. I forced myself on you."

"It didn't seem that way to me."

"Well, no," she said, "not once we got here—but you know what I mean. You don't have to pretend you're interested in me."

"But I am—you know, you can be a very exasperating young woman."

She smiled and said, "I know. It's part of my charm."

"Is that what you call it?"

She just grinned at him.

By the end of breakfast he had asked her many questions, and assured her many times that he was interested in her, and interested in seeing her again. He finally decided that, while she may have been inexperienced in bed, she certainly was not inexperienced out of bed.

They walked to the front door together and he put her in a cab.

"Will you be at the performance tonight?"

"I don't know. It will depend on how the day goes."

"Well," she said, "I'm at the Carlyle Hotel. Room fourteen."

"Room fourteen," he said. "I'll remember."

"You don't have to—"

"I'll remember," he said, and shouted to the driver, "take her to the Carlyle . . . quick."

He took his own cab to police headquarters and met Detective Eddie Spender at his desk.

"Heard you had some excitement last night."

"Where did you hear that from?"

"Downstairs."

"Downstairs? What's downstairs?"

"Oh, sorry," Spender said. "The cells. They still have your man in custody downstairs. I think they're waiting for word from you before they cut him loose."

"Why me? I didn't have him locked up, the commissioner did."

"Commissioner's not in," Spender said, "and you were there. Somebody's got to okay his release."

"Okay, fine," Clint said. "Release him."

Spender grinned. "Let's take a walk downstairs and you can tell them that yourself."

TWENTY-FIVE

They went down to where the big man from the night before was being held.

"I don't need to see him," Clint said to the guard. "Just let him go." He was sure that the man was just an avid—maybe too avid—fan of Grace's. You couldn't lock up a man and throw away the key for that.

"Ever get a name on him?" Spender asked.

"No," the guard said, "he wasn't talking when he came in. Funny thing, though."

"What's that?" Spender asked.

"He kept throwing himself at the bars, like he thought he could knock them down."

"He's a pretty big man," Clint said. "How long did that go on?"

"Hours. For a while, there, I thought he was gonna do it. Then he just . . . stopped."

"Maybe he got tired," Clint said.

"No, sir," the guard said, "every time I checked him he was wide awake. I don't think he slept a wink the whole night."

Under other circumstances Clint might have taken the time to talk to the man, but they were after something much bigger than a lovesick fan—no matter how big he was.

"Let him go," Clint said. "Maybe he'll go home and get some sleep."

"Yes, sir."

Clint and Spender left the area before Dimitri was released, so that neither one saw him that morning.

When he was released Dimitri went right to his residential hotel, where he had one room. He took a bath, got dressed, and hurried to Dr. Henry Cecil's clinic for work. He was going to have to explain the fact that he was a full hour late, and he didn't want to tell the doctor that he'd been in jail.

He'd have to come up with something.

Clint spent the morning being taken around to the scenes of the crimes by Eddie Spender. They started first with just the cemeteries, and then the scenes of all the murders.

They got to the cemeteries in the morning, and then stopped for lunch before going on to the murder scenes. Spender, who seemed to know every inch of the city, found a decent place to eat and Clint attempted to get to know the man a little better by asking questions.

"When did you know you wanted to be a detective?"

"I always knew."

"What else did you ever do?"

"Not much."

"What do you do when you're not working?"

"Not much."

It didn't take long for Clint to realized that Eddie Spender did not like talking about himself—at all. He could respect that, though. He didn't much like talking about himself—about the man people thought he was, anyway.

To his credit, while Spender didn't talk a lot and answered questions about himself with one word or less, neither did he ask too many personal questions.

He did, however, answer in detail any questions Clint had about the crimes, the crime scenes, or the city.

After lunch they went out to see the scenes of the last two murders.

"You know this city amazingly well," Clint said, on the way there.

"I make a point of knowing it well," Spender said. "I was born here, and I like it. I want to keep it the way I like it."

"I don't know any one place as well as you know this one."

"Maybe not," Spender said, "but I'll bet you've been to a lot more places than I have."

"I do travel a lot."

"New York?"

"Yes."

"How about Europe?"

"I've been there."

"Where else?" Spender was showing his first inkling of interest in Clint's personal life.

"I've been to Australia, South America, Canada . . ."

Spender nodded and said, "I haven't even heard of all those places. I'd like to go someplace, though . . . some day."

"Why don't you?"

"It takes money," Spender said, "and I didn't exactly pick a career where I can make a lot of money, you know?"

"I know," Clint said. "I was a lawman years ago, and you can't make a lot of money wearing a badge—"

"Don't I know it."

"—not legally, anyway."

Spender gave Clint a slow look.

"I'd never do anything illegal while I was wearing my badge," he said, slowly. "Never."

"Eddie," Clint said, "I never meant to imply that you would."

"I just want to make that clear," Spender said. "I take this job and the badge very seriously." He looked at Clint again. "Did they give you a badge?"

"Yes."

"Where is it?"

"In my pocket."

"Be proud of it."

"I'm sure it's something to be very proud of, Eddie," Clint said. "This one just happened to be given to me for convenience, so I'd have it to show when I was asking questions."

"That's what I'd like to start doing," Spender said.

"What?"

"Asking somebody questions . . . anybody!"

"We will," Clint said, "as soon as we figure out who."

TWENTY-SIX

Dr. Cecil was very upset with Dimitri for being late.

"I am sorry, Doctor," Dimitri said, when he arrived. "I . . . have no excuse for my lateness."

"Then I should have no excuse for not paying you for the day," Cecil said.

"No, sir."

"I don't pay you to come in late."

"No, sir."

Cecil regarded the big man for a moment, could not deny a wave of affection for him. Dimitri was sometimes like a large child and, truth be told, he was intensely loyal to Cecil, who was only five or six years older.

"I will pay you for the day, Dimitri," he said, relenting, "but I will deduct one hour."

"That is fair, Doctor."

"We have to get ready for tonight," Cecil said. "You will have to make a pickup and bring it back here."

"Yes, sir."

"I will be waiting by the back door, as usual."

"Yes, sir."

"You remember where to make the pickup?"

"Yes, Doctor."

"Very well," Cecil said. "Do your day's work, then. I will be in my laboratory."

"Yes, sir."

Dimitri watched as Cecil walked to the door of his laboratory, went inside, and locked the door behind him. Dimitri was only allowed inside when there were pickups or deliveries made—like tonight.

Dimitri was impressed by Henry Cecil. He was impressed with his intelligence, his confidence, and his money. Also, were it not for the doctor, Dimitri knew he would have been in jail a long time ago. He didn't like jail. He'd been there a few times, including last night—although last night was his first time in an American jail. He'd been very careful since arriving in America, and it had only been his passion for Grace Abbott that had caused him to be careless last night. He paid the price by spending the night in jail, but someone else was going to pay a bigger price.

He simply had to find a way to see his own business without letting it take him away from his job.

Dimitri fetched a broom and began to sweep. Keeping the clinic clean was one of his jobs, and even though there had never been a patient in the place, he made sure to sweep it every day. After sweeping he would dust, and then polish, and then he would get rid of the garbage—if the doctor had generated any. Sometimes it was normal garbage, papers and cans and other discarded objects—but sometimes the discarded "object" was much larger, and unusual. Sometimes an animal, but sometimes more. The doctor had not generated that kind of garbage in a couple of weeks, but he knew that with the pickup he was making tonight, he soon would.

Very soon.

TWENTY-SEVEN

By the end of the day Clint knew he was just marking time. He had seen all the crime sites, and had no ideas. He felt as if he was wasting everyone's time—George Karl's, Detective Spender's, even the mayor's.

"Hey," Spender said.

"What?"

They were in the buggy heading back to police headquarters.

"We forgot to look in the newspaper today."

"What?"

"The newspaper," Spender said. "The *Plain Dealer*. We forgot to look for the story on you."

"That's right, we did."

First chance he got Spender reined in the lone horse pulling their buggy and went into a store to buy a copy of the newspaper. He came out, handed it to Clint, and started the horse moving again.

Clint didn't have to look far to find the story. It was right there on page one, for all to see.

GUNSMITH JOINS HUNT FOR KILLER!

"Great," he said.

"Like it?"

"No."

Spender looked puzzled.

"But you agreed to it, didn't you?"

"I had to agree to some publicity," Clint said. "My name—my real name—doesn't appear anywhere."

"Are you sure?"

Clint took the time to read the article. It said the famous legend of the west, the Gunsmith, had joined the Cleveland Police Department as a special consultant to try to aid in the apprehension of the heinous killer who had been terrorizing the city for the past few months.

"Nope," Clint said, "doesn't appear."

"Then they kept their bargain?"

"Apparently."

"What a surprise."

"Why?"

"In my experience," Spender said, "newspapers and newspaper people are out only for themselves, and to sell newspapers. They hardly ever keep a bargain when it comes to printing something."

"Could it be the mayor's influence?" Clint asked.

"No doubt about it," Spender said. "The mayor has a lot of friends in this city. The editor of the newspaper is one of them."

When they reached police headquarters Clint said, "I better check in with the commissioner."

"Especially since you only have to check in with him," Spender said. "I'll be at my desk."

Clint nodded. The two men went up the stairs together and separated in the hall. Clint went down to George Karl's door and entered. Addy was seated behind her desk, but seemed to be preparing to leave.

"Hello, Mr. Adams," she said. "He's inside. You can go right in."

"Thank you, Addy. Finished for the day?"

"Yes, sir," she said, standing, "but it's only my workday

that is finished. Now I must go home and tend to personal things."

Clint thought to ask what personal things, but Addy seemed to him to be a very private person, so he decided not to.

"Well, have a nice evening, then, and I'll see you tomorrow."

"Good-night, sir."

Addy left and Clint went to Karl's door, knocked, and entered when the commissioner called out, "Come!"

As Clint came into the room Karl said, "I hope you have some good news for me, like the killer tracked you down and turned himself in to you."

"Afraid not," Clint said. He plopped into a chair and dropped the newspaper on Karl's desk.

"Yeah, I saw the paper," Karl said. "Played it up big, didn't they?"

"Big enough," Clint said, with an unhappy scowl.

"Well, how did you and Spender get along?"

"We got along fine," Clint said. "We didn't find out a lot, or come up with any new ideas, but we got along okay."

"That's a good start, anyway," Karl said. "He really doesn't get along well with the others."

"Maybe he's too good."

"You think so?"

"I don't know," Clint said. "I can't tell after spending one day with him. You seem pretty impressed with him, though.

"I am," Karl said, "and I think you will be, too, once you've spent some more time with him."

"I'll let you know." Clint put his hands on his knees, preparing to stand. "I think I'll head for my hotel, and dinner."

"Dinner," Karl said. "That reminds me. Walt Coburn asked me to have you stop in and see him when you got back."

"What does he want?"

"I don't know," Karl said. "Maybe he wants to have that dinner with you."

"Well," Clint said, standing, "I'll go ahead and stop by. Guess I'll see you in the morning."

"Not going to the play tonight?"

"I saw it once," Clint said. "That's enough."

"What about Grace? Won't she be disappointed?"

"I don't know," Clint said, "will she?"

"Hey," Karl said, "you know her better than I do. I thought you two were . . . friendly."

"I found out she's also 'friendly' with her director."

"Him?" Karl was surprised.

"Yes," Clint said, "seems he's a ladies' man. Sleeps with all his leading ladies."

"And where did you find this out?"

"A little bird told me."

"Maybe the little bird has a motive of her own for telling a story like that?" Karl suggested.

"No," Clint said, "I saw them last night. It's no story."

"And you don't like to share?"

"Not women," Clint said, "or ammunition. Good-night, George."

"Night, Clint."

Clint left, walked down the hall and entered the chief of detective's office. Apparently, his girl had left for the day, as well. He walked to the chief's door and knocked.

"Come on in."

He opened it and walked in. Coburn was behind his desk, his sleeves rolled up over his forearms, which were powerful.

"Ah, Adams, glad you could stop by," Coburn said. "I was hoping we could share that dinner tonight, maybe get acquainted."

"I don't see why not," Clint said, "but I'd like to stop by my hotel and freshen up first."

"That's no problem," Coburn said. "Would you like to eat there?"

"I'll leave that up to you, since it's your town," Clint said.

"I'll stop by at seven, then?"

"That's fine. See you then, Chief."

"Walt," Coburn said, "just call me Walt."

"All right, Walt," Clint said. "You can call me Clint."

"I'll see you at seven, Clint."

Clint nodded and left the chief of detective's office, wondering what the man had in mind besides dinner.

TWENTY-EIGHT

Clint went back to his hotel and took full advantage of the modern plumbing in his room. He was able to take a long leisurely bath without needing someone to come in and pour a bucket of water over him every few minutes. Prowling around cemeteries and murder scenes had made him feel particularly dirty, and he didn't step out of the bath until he felt clean.

He went into the bedroom and looked at the bed. He'd had two different women there with him the past two nights. The sheets, however, were clean and crisp, evidence of a maid's presence. He dressed in fresh clothes and checked his watch. He had time for a drink in the hotel bar before Walt Coburn stopped by.

He entered the bar and was impressed. It certainly matched the opulence of the Saxon Hotel's lobby, and dining room. He went to the long, mahogany bar and ordered a beer from one of the two bartenders. They were both impeccable in white shirts, vests, and ties. The man who brought him his beer was in his thirties, while the other bartender seemed a decade younger.

"Isn't he young for a bartender?" Clint asked, about the other man.

"I'm training him," the man said.

"How's he doing?"

"He'll never get the hang of it," the barman said. "I had another one in here last week, and there'll be a different one next week. All the same age. Where have all the decent bartenders gone?"

"Still out west, I guess."

"You said it, friend," the bartender said. "Sometimes I wish I never left Dodge City."

"When were you in Dodge?"

"A few years ago," the man said, "during one of the quieter periods in its history. I decided to go east and make my fortune. This was as far as I got."

"This looks pretty good."

"Oh, don't get me wrong," the man said. "This is a great place to work, but I'm still gonna move further east."

"New York?"

"That's where I want to end up. Ever been there?"

"Sure have," Clint said. "Nice saloons and bars, good bartenders."

"Well, I don't want to be a bartender all my life, either."

"Oh? Got something else in mind?"

"Yep," the man said. "Want to be a writer. That's why I want to go to New York. That's where publishing is."

Clint became wary. He didn't want to tell the bartender his name, now that he knew he was a fledging writer. He'd had that problem before, of writers wanting to write his story. He figured it was time to go and wait for Coburn in the lobby.

"Well, thanks for the beer," Clint said. "Good luck getting to New York."

"Thanks. Ain't gonna happen for a few years, but it's gonna happen, I can tell you that."

Clint waved and left. As he went out the door he heard the older bartender yelling at the other, "No, that ain't the way I showed you to do it . . ."

 • • •

Dr. Henry Cecil sat in his laboratory, reading the newspaper Dimitri had brought him, drinking a cup of tea. This Gunsmith the paper talked about intrigued him. He knew he had heard the name before—and then he remembered. Several years back, in London, a strangler had been loose and this Gunsmith had been there. He'd been attending a gun expo, and had been instrumental in finally catching the man.

And now he was in Cleveland.

Cecil put the paper down and picked up his cup. He sipped slowly while he considered what this might mean. Certainly, it was coincidence that found them both in Cleveland at the same time, but while he had some knowledge of the Gunsmith, the man certainly had no knowledge of him. No, at the moment the man did not appear to be a threat to him.

Abruptly, there was a knock at the back door. It was Dimitri, returning from making his pickup. Cecil put down his cup and went to unlock the back door to allow Dimitri to bring his burden in.

While waiting in the lobby for Coburn to appear Clint did some innocent people watching. It was something he had only recently begun to do, especially in train stations or hotels. It was interesting to watch perfect strangers moving about and to create personalities, histories, and goals for them.

The clientele of the Saxon was very high class indeed, but Clint could swear that he saw one or two couples where the woman was a working girl, even here at the Saxon Hotel. They were with men much too old and ugly for them, held too tight and pressed too close for them to be an actual couple. He felt sure that if he sat there for another hour he might see the couples leave again, or perhaps even the women leaving on their own. Then again, he saw no unescorted women in the lobby of the hotel, so the customers would probably have to walk the women out so as not to arouse suspicion.

He was watching one such couple walk by when Walt Coburn approached him.

"Yeah, that happens even here," Coburn said.

"Why not do something about it?" Clint asked, standing up.

"Not my department," Coburn said. "The chief of detectives doesn't round up whores. Do you like steak?"

"I love steak."

"I have a place in mind, but we'll have to ride a little way. I have a carriage and driver out front. Do you mind?"

"Not at all," Clint said. "As I said, it's your town."

"I've only been here a short time," Coburn said, as they walked to the door, "so I don't know it at all that well, but I do know this place."

"You still know it better than I do," Clint said. "You lead, I'll follow."

"Very well," Coburn said, and they went out the door.

TWENTY-NINE

It was dark and the streets looked pretty much the same to Clint, so he decided to stop trying to figure out where they had gone from the hotel. Instead, he settled back and waited until they reached their destination.

Coburn also rode in silence, preferring to reserve conversation until they reached the restaurant.

When they got there Coburn said, "We're here." He stepped out first, then waited for Clint. "Come back in two hours," he told the driver, who nodded and drove off. He noticed Clint watching him and said, "I don't like to rush my dinner."

"I can see that."

"Come on," Coburn said, "they're holding a table."

They approached the front of a well-lit restaurant. Backlit through the window was the name Delcorso's Steak House.

As they entered a man in a black suit hurried to greet Coburn by name and by rank.

"Chief Coburn, how nice to see you."

"Nice to see you, too, Nico. Is my table ready?"

"But of course, Chief. Always. Please, follow me."

The man led them through a tangle of tables, all occupied by two, three, or more people. Clint did not see one table

117

with only a single person seated. Also, there seemed to be an equal number of women and men.

They reached a table that was against a wall, with a reserved sign on it. Nico removed the sign and tucked it beneath his arm.

"Your table, gentlemen," he said, with a magnanimous grin. Clint had the definite feeling the man was putting on an act—but maybe he did it with everyone, and not just policemen. "What can we get you to drink?"

"A brandy for me," Coburn said. "Clint?"

"Beer."

"Excellent," Nico said. "I will send your waiter over to take your dinner order."

"No rush, Nico," Coburn said. "The drinks first."

"Of course," Nico said. "Immediately."

As the man rushed away Clint asked, "Come here often?"

It was a joke, but Walt Coburn did not seem to have a sense of humor.

"I try to come as often as I can," Coburn said. "A friend brought me here soon after I arrived in Cleveland, and I haven't found a better restaurant, yet. Wonderful steaks."

"Sounds good."

"Excellent brandy, too," Coburn said. "I, uh, discovered brandy when I took this job. It seemed to fit my position better than beer."

"I suppose."

"But you go ahead and have beer."

"I will."

The waiter appeared with their drinks, greeting Coburn as "Chief," and saying how good it was to see him.

"You too, Angelo."

"Enjoy your drinks," Angelo said. "I'll come back when you're ready to order dinner."

"Thank you, Angelo."

Clint picked up his beer and took a swallow. It was ice cold and felt good going down.

"So," Coburn said, "how was your first day?"

"Tiring," Clint said. "I guess visiting cemeteries can do that to you."

"I can imagine," Coburn said. "How did you and Spender get along?"

"Well."

"Really?" Coburn asked.

"Why is that surprising?"

"He doesn't get along with anyone else," Coburn said. "Karl—the commissioner—hired him against my recommendation."

"Really? I seemed to have no trouble getting along."

"That's odd," Coburn said.

"Of course," Clint said, "it could just be that I'm also difficult to get along with."

"Really? I hadn't heard that about you."

Clint decided then and there to save his jokes. They would obviously be wasted on this man.

"Oh, I see," Coburn said, as if reading Clint's mind, "you were joking. I'm sorry, I suppose I don't have much of a sense of humor—especially when my city is in the grips of some crazy killer."

Oh boy, Clint thought. This went beyond a lack of a sense of humor.

"Your city?"

Coburn smiled a little sheepishly.

"I'm afraid I've come to think of it that way," he said. "You see, I like it here. It's not my adopted home, but I'm very protective of it."

"Well, that's understandable."

"What did you and Spender do today?"

"As I said, we visited cemeteries," Clint said. "I had him take me to all the crime scenes—the graveyards and the murder sites."

"Ah," Coburn said, "and what did that accomplish?"

"It simply familiarized me with the markings on his map."

"Ah," Coburn said, "Spender's famous map. I don't have much use for it, myself."

"Really?" Clint asked. "I thought it was an excellent idea. I asked the commissioner about getting one made up, and he told me that Spender had already done it. It seems we were thinking along the same lines right away."

"Hmm," Coburn said, "interesting."

"Chief . . . Walt . . . can we cut through the bull here?"

"I'm sorry?" Coburn stopped with his brandy glass half-way to his mouth.

"Why did you really ask me to come to dinner?" Clint asked. "Were you afraid I'd already found something out?"

"Why would I be afraid of such a thing?" Coburn asked. "For one thing, I want this killer caught. Anything you might find out would be helpful. But secondly—and more importantly—I don't expect you to find anything out."

"And why not?"

"Well . . . and no offense intended . . . you don't know the city, and you are not a detective, no matter what Commissioner Karl thinks."

"Well," Clint said, "it's very hard for me to argue with either of those points, isn't it?"

"I'm glad you see it my way," Coburn said. "May I tell you how I see your role here?"

"Please do."

"I think you can sit back and relax, look busy, take whatever money the city is paying you, and stay out of the way while me and my men catch this killer."

"Your men, including Spender?"

"Spender is a maverick," Coburn said. "He won't work with the others. On his own he won't get much done. I'm afraid he won't be in on the final capture, either."

"You sound like you're closing in on your man, Chief."

"Well, we have some leads—"

"Well, I know differently."

"I beg your pardon?"

"I know that you're baffled, stymied, stumped, whatever

you want to call it. You have no leads. If you did, I wouldn't be here. If you did the mayor wouldn't have bothered planting a story about me in the newspaper."

Coburn scowled.

"That was idiotic. Does he really expect the killer to be frightened and just leave the city? I doubt it!"

"You see?" Clint said. "We agree again. The way I see my role, Chief, is to maybe act as a liaison between you and your own man, Spender. You see, I think he just might have what it takes to solve this thing."

"Based on what?"

Based on nothing, Clint thought. At the moment he was just trying to get the man's goat.

"Observation, and instinct. I observed his methods today. I like the way his mind works. It's logical."

"And instinct?"

"I have a good feeling about him."

"And you don't about me?"

"I think you have the same problem George Karl has."

"Which is what?"

"Which is you were once both good detectives but you've now become politicians. You're too busy playing the political game in Cleveland to be able to do what you've always done."

"And what is that?" Coburn asked, stiffly.

"Detect, man," Clint said. "You and George used to detect."

"What do you know about me?"

"I know that if you worked with Jim Hume you must have been good."

Coburn turned his brandy glass around in his hand, staring at it.

"Past tense?" he asked, finally.

"You tell me," Clint said. "You know what's going on in your head a lot better than I do."

He waited while Coburn played the situation over in his

head. Finally, the man came to a decision and put his glass down.

"Mr. Adams," he said, "I think perhaps this dinner was a bad idea. If you go out front there is a doorman there who will get you a cab back to your hotel."

"I'm sorry you feel that way, Chief."

"I do."

Clint stood up.

"Maybe tomorrow you'll feel different."

"I doubt it."

The two men stared at each other for a few more moments, and then Clint turned and left.

THIRTY

Getting back to his hotel was no problem. When he entered the room he sniffed the air, but did not detect any perfume. Apparently, he was not going to be sharing it with a woman tonight. Both Grace and Sherrill would be either on stage or backstage tonight, and he doubted that either one would show up afterward.

Later, he'd find out how wrong he was.

Dimitri knew very little of what Dr. Henry Cecil's work really was. All he did was make pickups, or arrange for deliveries.

As Cecil held the door open he carried the pickup into the room and set it on the examination table.

"Is it fresh?" Cecil asked.

"Very fresh."

It was wrapped in a blanket. Cecil unwrapped it and looked down at it. It was female, young, in its twenties. He touched the arms and legs and found them loose, not yet stiff.

"Yes, yes," he said, "good . . . very fresh. Where is the . . . ah, there it is."

The killing blow had been to the head, caving in the skull. He was worried that the brain may have been damaged. If it had been, he wasn't going to pay the rest of the money. However, the blow—upon second examination—did not seem to have done great damage to the skull, other than killing the subject.

"All right, Dimitri," he said, "you can go."

"Yes, sir."

"But stay around," Cecil said. "I don't know what time I'll be quitting tonight."

"Yes, sir."

Dimitri walked to the door, but even before he had gone through it he was forgotten.

Rachel was late getting home, and her mother was extremely worried, especially with this killer roaming about. Although her daughter was twenty-two—an adult—her mother still worried as if she were a child. She was usually home from work an hour ago. This was not like her.

She decided to call the police.

When the first knock came at the door Clint had no idea who it could be. When he opened it he saw Sherrill standing there.

"Is the play over?" he asked.

"No," she said, sashaying into the room, "but they won't need me tonight. No room for the understudy."

He closed the door and turned to face her. She was smiling, but there was also something tentative about her, as if she wasn't quite sure he would let her stay.

"Do you mind me stopping by?" she asked.

"No, not at all."

"What did you do today?"

"Just tried to familiarize myself with the city."

She walked around, touching things without really seeing them.

"I was hoping you'd be here," she said, "and that you wouldn't mind me coming."

"Sherrill—"

"I mean," she said, "I'm not trying to be a pest, or anything . . ."

"You're not a pest."

"I'm not?"

"No."

"Then . . ." she said, and turned to look at the bedroom.

"I was just thinking about that," he said.

She smiled and started for the bedroom, her fingers already busy on the buttons of her dress. As Clint started to follow, though, there was another knock on the door. Sherrill reached the doorway of the bedroom and turned, her dressed partially open, exposing her breasts.

Clint opened the door. It was Detective Eddie Spender. He looked past Clint and saw Sherrill, who hurriedly closed her dress.

"I'm sorry," Spender said. "I didn't mean to interrupt anything."

"What's wrong?"

"We got a call about a missing young woman," he said. "I'm going out to her house, thought you might like to come along."

"You think the killer struck again?"

"I think," Spender said, "we just have to look into every possibility."

"All right," Clint said. "I'll be right down."

Spender nodded, took one last look at Sherrill, and then started back down the hall. Clint closed the door and turned to face her.

"I've got to go."

"Can I wait?"

"I don't know how long I'll be."

"I'll wait, if it's okay."

"It's fine," he said.

His New Line was on a table by the door. He retrieved it, tucked it into his belt and put on his jacket.

"Good luck," she said.

"Thanks," he said, and hurried out the door.

* * *

Down in the lobby Spender once again said, "Sorry to interrupt."

"No problem. How did you find out about this girl?"

"Her mother reported her missing to the police. We've let it be known at all the police stations that we want to know about anybody who comes up missing, and as soon as possible. The mother says this girl was an hour late coming home from work."

"Does she have a boyfriend?"

"No, and she's never late."

"So if she was grabbed that recently she's probably still alive."

"Maybe," Spender said, as they went out the front door. "If he sticks to his pattern she might turn up dead three or four days from now."

"But that won't mean she wasn't dead all this time."

"Right."

"What does he do with them?" Clint wondered aloud, as they reached the carriage. "I mean, first buried dead bodies, and then fresh ones. Could he be . . . experimenting on them?"

"What do you mean?"

They got in and the carriage started moving.

"I mean," Clint said, "is this some . . . medical thing."

"You think a doctor is doing this?"

"Who needs bodies?" Clint asked. "Don't they use them at medical schools to teach medicine?"

"Well, yeah, but—"

"It's just a thought."

They rode in silence for a few moments, and then Spender said, "A gruesome one."

THIRTY-ONE

They stopped at the mother's house and got the girl's name, Rachel Bennett. From there they went to her place of business, a dress shop that was closed for the day, but the owner lived upstairs. They questioned the owner, an older woman named Mrs. Holden, who said that Rachel left the same time she always left. She didn't see or hear anything out of the ordinary.

Clint and Spender left the old woman's apartment and stood in front of the dress shop.

"I guess all we can do now is walk her route home," Spender said, so that's what they did.

It was about a fifteen minute walk, but when they arrived at the house Clint noticed that across the street there was a small cemetery.

"Eddie."

"What?"

"Look."

"So?" Spender said, "A cemetery. This one was taken alive, Clint."

"No, that's not what I mean," Clint said. "Look at the route we walked to get here. If she cut through that cemetery she'd save time."

Spender looked at him and said, "You're right. Let's take a look."

They crossed the street and entered the little graveyard. The stones were very old, and there didn't look to be any new graves. Obviously, it had not been used to bury a loved one—or anyone—in a long time.

The moon was bright and they had plenty of light to see by, which was why Clint noticed a patch of something black on one of the headstones.

"Eddie."

Spender turned his head and saw Clint leaning over the stone.

"What is it?" he asked.

Clint looked at him.

"It looks black in the moonlight," Clint said, "but it's blood."

Further search of the graveyard with torchlights yielded some evidence of a struggle near the bloodstained headstone. In the end it appeared someone had been dragged from the graveyard and then possibly lifted onto a buggy or buckboard.

"See the track?" Clint said, getting down on one knee. "Her heels dragged in the dirt, and then here are the tracks of the wheels of the buggy, or whatever."

"The tracks are no good," Spender complained. "You can't follow wagon tracks over cobblestone streets."

"Well," Clint said, "it's pretty sure someone was cutting through the cemetery and was assaulted, maybe killed, and then removed."

"Too much coincidence for it not to be this Rachel," Spender said. "What do we tell her mother about this?"

"Let's not tell her anything about it," Clint said. "There's no need for the mother to get upset, or believe that her daughter's dead, until the body actually shows up."

"Okay, but what do we do?" Spender asked.

"We could come back tomorrow, around the time the girl

usually left work, follow the path she took, and ask some questions. Maybe somebody saw something."

"I suppose."

"Hey, Eddie," Clint said, "this abduction is our only lead. Let's not let the trail get too cold on us."

"You're right," Spender said. "Okay, then, I guess we better get going, then. We can meet at headquarters tomorrow, fill the commissioner and the chief in on what happened, and what we're planning to do about it."

"Okay," Clint said, "but let's just stop in on the mother tonight and tell her . . . well, something."

"Let's just tell her we're still looking," Spender said.

"Good idea."

They left the graveyard and headed back to Rachel Bennett's house.

When Clint turned the key in the lock of his hotel door and opened it he didn't expect to find what he found. Sitting in one of the overstuffed chairs was Grace Abbott. As he entered she turned and gave him a stony look.

"If you're looking for your little friend," she said, "she's in the bedroom."

She was obviously angry, and he really didn't want to have to deal with that, now. He walked to the bedroom door and saw Sherrill in the bed, awake and staring at him.

"She showed up shortly after you left, and she wouldn't leave until she talked to you."

"Are you all right?"

"I'm fine," she said. "Do you want me to leave?"

"No," Clint said, "just stay right there until I get this all sorted out."

He turned and went back into the other room.

THIRTY-TWO

"If you'd wanted an understudy you should have said so," Grace Abbott said to him, haughtily, as she got to her feet. "How do you think I felt, rushing over here after the performance and finding her here?"

"I don't have time for this Grace," Clint said. "You're acting like a wife who's been cheated on."

"You've got the cheating part right."

"No, I don't," he said. "What about you and your director?"

"David?"

"That's his name, isn't it? You're sleeping with him, aren't you?"

She turned her head away.

"What's that got to do with anything?"

"It's got plenty to do with everything," Clint said. "If you're already involved in a relationship with a man then I don't need to become your man on the side."

"You're not on the side," she said. "I'm just sleeping with David because he sleeps with all his leading ladies."

"So you had to make sure his reputation stayed intact?"

"He—"

"Wait a minute," he said. "Are you telling me that you have to sleep with him to keep this part?"

She didn't answer.

"But . . . that's ridiculous. You're a great actress."

"I'm just an actress, Clint," she said. "He's a great director. Working with him might finally make me a great actress."

"And sleeping with him."

"Never mind," Grace said. "You have to make a choice."

"*I* have to make a choice? What about you?"

"You don't expect me to choose between you and my career, do you?" she asked. "We don't know each other that well."

"But you want me to choose, huh?"

"Well, you only have to choose between me," she said, "and an understudy."

"Sherrill is not just an understudy," he said, "she's a woman."

"Apparently, you've had both of us this week," she said. "You can still call her a woman after having been with me?"

"You're both women," he said.

"I don't even see how you can say that."

"Grace," Clint said, "I think for the remainder of your run here, you should concentrate on your performances—on stage, and in your director's bed."

She stared at him in disbelief.

"Are you choosing that . . . that understudy over me?"

"I'm afraid so," he said. "I'm afraid that your run here at the Saxon Hotel is over."

"Well!" She put her hands on her hips. "You'll be sorry you made this choice, Clint Adams."

She picked up her purse and stalked toward the door, stopping with her hand on the doorknob.

"And don't think I'll be leaving any more front-row tickets for you."

"That's all right," Clint said. "If you've seen one Lady Macbeth, you've seen them all."

"Oh!" she said, and stormed out, slamming the door behind her.

Sherrill appeared in the bedroom doorway.

"That was the thing you said that insulted her the most, you know."

He looked at her and said, "You know, I could use a drink."

"What happened tonight?"

He told her about the missing girl, and how he and Spender figured out that if she wasn't dead, she soon would be.

"You could use a drink," she said. "Why don't you go downstairs and get one? Or two?"

"You don't mind?"

"I'll wait here," she said. "I don't mind."

"You could get some sleep while I'm downstairs," he said. "You have to go to work tomorrow."

"Oh, I don't think I'll be going to work tomorrow."

"Why not?"

"After tonight I don't think I'll have a job in the theater tomorrow."

"Oh," he said, "I didn't realize . . . I'm sorry, Sherrill. I guess it's because of me, then."

"No, that's okay," she said. "I was tired of being an understudy, anyway."

"But you traveled all the way here with the show, and now to get fired—"

"I didn't travel far," she said. "I live here."

"What?"

"Didn't I tell you?" she asked. "I'm local. They hired me after I auditioned the first day. I heard about it and came here from Chagrin Falls."

"Chagrin Falls?"

"A small town just outside of Cleveland. It's beautiful. You should come and see our falls while you're here."

"Maybe I will," he said. "It's such a pretty name."

She came walking over to him, wearing only a slip of underwear. If he wasn't thinking about a dead girl the little humps her nipples made in the material would surely have lured him into bed.

She took his arm and said, "You go down and have a drink or two and come back when you're ready. And when you come back, if all you want to do is sleep, that'll be okay with me."

"You're a very understanding young lady," he said, kissing her nose. "And pretty, too."

"I can afford to be understanding," she said. "After all, you picked me over a famous stage actress tonight. I don't have to be anybody's understudy anymore."

She walked him to the door and opened it for him. It was as if she was seeing him off for a day at work.

"Just don't come back stinking drunk," she warned him. "If you fall on the floor I'm just going to leave you there."

"I'll remember," he said. "I just have to do some thinking, that's all. I'll be back soon."

"It's your room," she reminded him. "Come back when you're good and ready."

He left the room, feeling sure he'd made the right choice tonight. Given the size of Grace's ego it was just too crowded in bed with her.

THIRTY-THREE

"Tonight?" Dimitri asked.

"That is what I said, Dimitri," Henry Cecil replied. "I want it out of here tonight."

"But . . . you never get rid of them the same night."

"This one is different," Cecil said.

"Where do I take it?"

"I don't care," Cecil said. "Take it out and dump it somewhere, bury it somewhere. I don't care. I just want it out of my clinic."

The "subject" of their discussion had been a disappointment to him. His experiment had gone awry and he blamed the subject, so he wanted it taken away that night.

"I will wait for you here," Cecil said. "Dispose of it, then come back and take me home. Understand?"

Dimitri squared his shoulders and said, "Yes, sir, I understand."

"Good," Cecil said. "Then get it done. I'm going to have a cup of tea. By the time I'm finished I want to find it gone."

"Yes, sir."

Dimitri watched as Cecil left the hall and went into the kitchen. The door to the laboratory was not only unlocked, it was slightly ajar. He walked to it and went inside. The

subject was on the table and it was a mess. Obviously, it
had been cut up, but something must have angered the doctor, because Dimitri had never seen one of the subjects this
cut up before.

He was going to have to be very careful not to leave any
of the subject behind.

Clint had two beers in the almost empty hotel bar. There
was one bartender on duty, and he didn't recognize the man
at all. That was good. He didn't want to have to deal with
a beginning bartender, or with one who wanted to be a
writer. He'd ordered a beer twice, and the only words the
bartender had said to him either time was, "Comin' up."

The man knew his job.

Clint, on the other hand, felt he didn't. No matter what
George Karl thought or said, no matter what he had agreed
to do, he did not know this job of being a detective. That
was Spender's business. Still, it had been Clint who had
found the blood and read the sign on the ground. At least
he had contributed in that fashion.

Tomorrow maybe he and Spender would be able to find
a witness. He had the feeling that, in the end, if this killer
was to be caught, somebody was going to have to have
seen something, and somebody was going to have to talk.

After a couple of hours—he couldn't believe he'd nursed
a beer an hour—he considered getting a third one or going
to his room. He finally decided to go back to the room.
There was a woman waiting for him there, a warm, willing
woman who would let him get lost in her flesh for the
whole night, before he had to go out tomorrow and possibly
tell a woman that her daughter was dead.

Spender sat in a chair with a glass of whiskey in his hand.
This business of leading two lives was beginning to get to
him. It had all started when he met Elvira. He had been
instantly drawn to her in a way he had never been drawn
to a woman before. When they met they were on opposite

ends of society, and he knew that if he was going to have her he was going to have to move to her side. Policeman by day, rogue by night, living with a whore, protecting her, plotting with her—and here he was. Halfway between Heaven and Hell, good and bad, need and desire.

He was going to have to make a choice, before he decided what to do about this doctor she was setting up. Scoring a large sum of money off him would set them up for a while, but did he really want to give up being a detective? He loved his job, but it made Elvira nervous. So he was going to have to choose, and choose soon.

Maybe, he thought, it could wait until after he caught this killer. Catch the killer, take the doctor, and then disappear with Elvira.

It sounded like a plan.

Elvira waited in Henry Cecil's bed, thinking not about the doctor, but about her man, the police detective. How had she ever let herself get involved with a man who was a policeman? What was wrong with her? Although he was part of her world, he came from the other side of it. Any other policeman would arrest her, not live with her. She knew that something was going on inside of Spender, and that he was going to have to make a decision very soon.

He was going to have to stop walking the line and pick one side, or the other.

THIRTY-FOUR

An insistant knocking on the door woke Clint the next morning. He had to disentangle himself from Sherrill's arms and legs to answer, and did so without waking her. She was a remarkably sound sleeper.

He walked to the door, pulling his trousers on at the same time. On the table next to the door was his Colt New Line. His gun and holster was still hanging on the bedpost. He picked up the New Line, held it behind his back, and opened the door.

"We found her," Spender said.

"Where?" Clint knew immediately who he meant.

"Get dressed," Spender said. "I'll wait downstairs and take you there."

"Ten minutes," Clint said.

"Make it five."

"Right."

He didn't even take time to leave Sherrill a note.

Her body was found in the same cemetery she had been abducted from. She was lying facedown in front of a headstone—a different one than the one they'd found her blood on. She was naked, but her clothes had been thrown on top of her, almost as an afterthought. When they turned her

139

over they saw that she was not altogether. Somebody had cut her up good.

"Jesus," Clint said when Spender lifted the blanket to show the girl to him. He had to swallow hard; he had seen some gruesome things in his life—but nothing like this. The fact that the girl was so young made it even worse.

"Who'd do that to a beautiful young girl, Clint?" Spender asked. He dropped the blanket back down over her.

"It looks messy, Eddie," Clint said, "but the cuts look neat."

"Sharp knife."

"And somebody who knew what they were doing."

"A doctor?"

Clint nodded.

"Jesus," Spender said. "Doctors are supposed to save lives, aren't they?"

"Most of them do," Clint said.

"How many don't?"

Clint looked down at the girl's body, shook his head, and said, "At least one, I guess."

"Who told the mother?" Commissioner Karl asked.

"I did," Spender said.

They were in Karl's office—Clint, Spender, and George Karl.

"How'd she take it?"

"How would you expect?"

There was a knock on the door and when Karl yelled, "Come!" chief of detectives Walt Coburn came in.

"Is what I heard true?" he asked.

"It's true, Chief," Spender said.

"Jesus," Coburn said, shaking his head. It was a moment when all four men had something in common—but the moment passed.

"Spender, why wasn't I notified?"

"Hadn't gotten to it yet, Chief," the detective said. "I

talked with the mother, and Clint came back to inform the commissioner."

"You would have been next, Walt," Karl said. "Take it easy."

"I've been working on this case as long as anyone," Coburn said. "I deserve to be notified right away."

"Have a seat, Walt."

Coburn ignored the invitation from the commissioner.

"Eddie," he said, "I'll be in my office. When you're done here I want a complete report. Understand?"

"I understand, Chief."

Coburn nodded shortly and then walked stiffly out.

"Maybe he'll fire me," Spender said.

"I don't think so, Eddie," Clint said.

"Nobody's getting fired," Karl said. "At least, not until this animal is caught. What about witnesses?"

"We left some men to try to find some," Clint said. "I guess Chief Carter's going to be upset he wasn't notified, either?"

"I'll take care of the chiefs," Karl said. "You two find me a killer. This is the first time we've gotten one so . . . fresh . . . excuse the term . . . and I don't want to waste this chance."

"Yes, sir," Spender said, "but I better go and talk to my chief."

"All right—" Karl started, but a knock at the door cut him off. He answered in his customary one word manner and it opened.

"Looking for Detective Spender, Comm—oh, there you are." It was a uniformed officer.

"Commissioner, this is Officer Bogart. We left him to look for witnesses." He looked at the man. "What's up, Sam?"

"We found one, Eddie," Bogart said. "At least, he says he saw something."

"You don't believe him?"

"He's downstairs in a cell," the man said. "He was arrested for being drunk and disorderly last night."

"What time?"

"I'm not sure," Bogart said, "but he's sayin' he saw something."

Spender looked at Clint.

"We better talk to him." Then he looked at Karl.

"Go ahead," the commissioner said. "Like I told you, I'll take care of the chiefs."

THIRTY-FIVE

The man's name was Bud Day. He was in his fifties, and the smell of liquor oozed from his pores. He had obviously been a drunk for a long time. Now, however, he was as close to sober as he'd ever be. He was jumpy, constantly rubbing his dry mouth with his hand.

"I need a drink," he said.

"After you tell us what we need to know, Bud," Spender said.

"About the girl?"

"That's right."

"I seen it."

"You saw what? The murder?"

"No," Day said, "the delivery."

Clint and Spender exchanged a glance.

"What delivery, Bud?"

"I seen the girl delivered to the big man."

"And where did this delivery take place."

"In the cemetery."

"Bud," Spender said, "you're going to have to be real specific."

"It was dark," Day said, "and I was sleepin' in the cemetery like I sometimes do. I heard some commotion, and then I seen him dragging the girl, so I followed him."

"A man dragging a girl," Spender said.

"Yes."

"Was she dead?"

"Musta been. She didn't put up no fight."

"She could have been knocked out."

"Coulda been," Day said, "but there was blood."

"Okay, Bud, so the man's dragging her . . . to where?"

"A road outside the cemetery."

"And what was there?"

"Big fancy carriage, and a big man waitin'."

"How big a man?" Spender asked. "Big as me? Or this man?" He pointed to Clint.

"Bigger'n both of you. Real big."

"Okay," Spender said, "so one man drags the girl through the cemetery and hands her off to the big man?"

"Right."

"And then what?"

"Well . . . the big man pays him."

"So the big man bought the dead girl from the other man?"

" 'S'right. Can I have a drink now?"

"In a few minutes, Bud," Spender said. "Do you know who the big man was?"

"No."

"Did you follow him?"

"No."

"So you didn't see where he took the girl?"

"No."

"Had you ever seen him before?"

"No."

Spender looked at Clint.

"What about the other man?" Clint asked. "The man you saw dragging the girl. Did you know him?"

"Oh sure."

"You did?" Spender asked.

"Yeah."

"Why didn't you tell me before?"

"You didn't ask me."

"Well, I'm asking you now," Spender said. "Who was the other man?"

"His name's Leo," Day said. "We drink together sometimes."

"Ever work together?"

"No."

"Why not?"

"I don't like the way he makes his money."

"And how's that?"

"Sellin' dead bodies," Day said, "like I just told you."

"Bud, where does he get the dead bodies he sells?"

"Digs 'em up."

"And does he have help?"

"Sometimes."

"And does he ever kill someone so that he can deliver their body?"

Day shrugged.

"You don't know?"

"No," Day said, "I just know that he digs 'em up sometimes."

"How does he know what bodies to dig up?" Spender asked.

"That's easy," Day said. "He buries them."

"So he's a grave digger?"

"Yup."

"And a grave robber?" Clint asked.

"Yup."

"But you never helped him with either?" Spender asked.

"No."

"Has he ever told you who he sells the bodies to?"

"No," Day said, "but I just tol' you I seen him sell it to that big man. Can I have a drink now?"

They were in a room on the first floor of the building, and the only other man in the room was Officer Bogart.

"Sam?"

Bogart produced a flask from his back pocket. It had

whiskey in it. He handed it over to Spender, who held it where Bud Day could see it.

"Bud, one more question."

Day said, "Uh-huh," without taking his eyes off the flask.

"Do you know where we can find Leo?"

"Sure."

"Where?"

Suddenly, Day's eyes became crafty and he said, "First I get the drink."

"Okay, Bud," Spender said, "A drink, and then the address. Right?"

Day nodded anxiously and said, "Right."

Spender gave him the flask.

THIRTY-SIX

After his drink Bud Day was able to tell them exactly where his friend Leo would be.

His name was Leo Haynes and he worked for the largest cemetery in Cleveland. When Clint and Spender got there Haynes and three other men were digging a hole into which someone's loved one would undoubtedly go. However, if Haynes needed a little extra money at any time, they had no doubt that he would dig the casket right back up again.

Haynes had the look of a drunk. Old clothes, beard stubble, body odor, but the odor of liquor did not quite leak from his pores the way it did from poor Bud Day's. Still, it was obvious that Leo Haynes was no stranger to the bottle—nor were the other two men he was working with, which made Clint and Spender wonder.

"You boys mind if we ask you a few questions?" Spender asked as the two men approached the three grave diggers.

"Who are ya?" Haynes asked. "You ain't supposed to be here while we's diggin', ya know."

"We can go anyplace we want, Leo," Spender said. He took out his badge. "We're the police."

The three men dropped their shovels and started running.

"Shit!" Spender said. "I'll get Leo, you get one of the others."

Clint didn't argue, because he and Spender were once again thinking along the same lines. If Haynes dug up bodies for money, and used help, then there was a good chance one of these other two men were his helpers.

While Spender took off after Leo Haynes, Clint saw that he had lucked out. The other two men were running off side by side, rather than being smart and splitting up about it. He took off after them, but he had no intention of running all day to catch them. He took out the Colt New Line and calmly put a bullet into one of their legs, simply picking one of the legs at random. It didn't matter to him who it belonged to.

One man yelled and went down as the bullet smacked him in the back of the thigh. The other man staggered, probably expecting to be hit when he heard the shot, then stopped running and turned, hands high. He took a moment to check and see if he was hit, and when he saw his friend writhing on the ground in pain he heaved a sigh of relief.

When Clint reached them the standing man said, "Don't shoot."

"Get on the ground."

The man obeyed.

"Either of you got a gun?"

"We don't got no guns," the uninjured man said. "Is he gonna bleed to death?"

"Maybe," Clint said.

"You gonna get him a doctor?"

"That depends."

"On what?"

"On whether or not you can tell me what I want to know," Clint said. "Also depends on whether or not my friend can catch your friend, Leo."

"You don't need to catch Leo," the man said. "We can tell you what you want to know."

The injured man wasn't even listening. He was blubbering and holding his thigh. Clint almost felt guilty about shooting him.

"What do you think I want to know?"

"You wanna know about the bodies we dug up and sold."

"That's part of it," Clint said, trying to hide his surprise at the fact that the man would talk so readily.

"What's the other part?"

"I want to know about the murders."

"Murders?" the man gasped. "Mister, we don't know nothing about no murders. We was just diggin' up bodies and sellin 'em to the doc."

"What doc?" Clint asked, his heart pounding. "You sold the bodies to a doctor?"

"Sure," the man said. "Who else would wanna buy dead bodies?"

"Who's the doctor?"

"Aw, hell, mister, we don't know no names. If you wanna know names then you do need Leo for that."

"And what about the murders?"

"I tol' you, we don't know about no murders."

"What about Leo?" Clint asked. "Will he know?"

"Maybe," the man said. "I wouldn't put it past Leo to do some killin' if there was some extra money in it. Is that what this is about? Leo's been killin' for extra money?"

"I don't know," Clint said. "I guess we'll have to wait and find out."

"He's gonna bleed to death," the man said, looking at his partner.

"Maybe," Clint said. "You should have thought of that before you started digging up bodies."

"We needed the money."

"For what? Whiskey?"

"It was Leo's idea," the man said. "He said we could make lots of money diggin' them up and sellin' them. He said nobody'd know."

"I guess he was wrong."

Clint turned when he heard someone behind him. Spender appeared, leading Leo ahead of him.

"I heard a shot," he said.

"I had to put a bullet into one of them to get them to stop," Clint said.

Spender pushed Leo over with the other two.

"This one says digging the bodies up and selling them was Leo's idea, but he says him and the other one don't know anything about murder."

"Damn it, Jenkins—" Leo snarled.

"I ain't goin' to jail for you, Leo," Jenkins, the uninjured man, said, "and Danny needs a doctor."

"You and him are gonna need more than a doctor if you double-cross me," Leo said, menacingly. Of course, he didn't have the physical presence to pull it off. Clint didn't even know how he had the strength to dig graves, he appeared to be so emaciated.

"Hey, Leo," Spender said, "you talk to me, now."

"You?" Leo said. "You're Spender, aïn'tcha?"

"That's right."

"I know all about you," he said. "You let me go or I'll start talkin'."

Clint frowned and looked at Spender.

"What's he talking about?"

"I don't know," Spender said, "and I don't think he does, either."

Spender walked over to Leo, pulled a cutdown Colt from inside his jacket and put it to the man's head.

"All I want to hear from you now is the answers to my questions, Leo," he said. "If I don't get them I'm going to leave your brains splattered all over this cemetery."

Leo tried to tough it out, but finally crumpled. "Whataya wanna know?" he asked, as his eyes started leaking.

THIRTY-SEVEN

"This is amazing," George Karl said.

"Clint had it figured," Spender said.

"But a doctor," Karl said, shaking his head.

They were in Commissioner Karl's office, filling him in on what they'd found out from Leo and his pals. In the room with Clint, Spender, and Commissioner Karl were both chiefs, Carter and Coburn.

"But none of them have admitted to the murders," Coburn pointed out.

"That's true," Clint said, "but two of them said it was Leo who did them, and delivered the bodies to the same man Bud Day saw—a huge man in an expensive carriage."

"But no names?" Karl asked.

"No," Spender said. "However, Leo was able to give us a description of the doctor because he met him on several occasions when the doctor was making it clear what he wanted."

"But the doctor himself never took delivery of a body," Clint said. "It was always the other man, the big one, whose description sounds familiar to me."

"Sounds like just another hulking brute," Chief Carter said.

"With one difference," Clint added.

"What's that?" Coburn asked.

"Well, Leo tried to describe the accent that both men spoke with, and it sounds to me like they were British."

"Wait a minute," Spender said, snapping his fingers. "The big man who gave you trouble at the theater."

"That's what I'm thinking," Clint said. "Would they have his name downstairs?"

"Might have his name and address," Spender said, standing up, "if they bothered to take them before they cut him loose."

Clint also stood up and said, "Let's find out."

They were out of luck. Since the man had been brought in and treated as a drunk he had simply been released the next morning—on the say-so of both Clint and Spender, the guard reminded them.

"Damn it!" Clint swore. They were now sitting at Spender's desk, with no one else in the room.

"How were we to know he was going to end up being involved with the murders?" Spender asked.

"But we had him in a cell," Clint said, shaking his head.

"We'll just have to find him again," Spender said, "him and the doctor he works for."

"Just like that?"

"No, not just like that," Spender said. "It'll take some work, but look how close we've come now. We've never been this close before."

"We can question the three grave diggers again," Clint said. "Maybe they'll reveal something they don't even know they know."

"It's worth a try," Spender said. "There's also got to be a way to check on doctors coming into Cleveland in the past year."

"Although if ours is a killer," Clint said, "I doubt that he'd register anyplace."

"Maybe he wasn't a killer when he got here," Spender said. "Maybe something happened to turn him into one."

"Doesn't hurt to check," Clint said, "but I don't think we'll find anything. We're going to have to find someone who can give him to us."

"One of the three grave diggers?"

"Leo," Clint said. "Leo's got to know more than he's telling."

"Well," Spender said, "there is one way to find out."

"How?"

"Let him go," Spender said, "and follow him. We can't prove he killed anybody."

"We've got a witness who saw him dragging *something* out of the cemetery and handing it over to *someone*. Do you think your chief, or the commissioner, will let you set him free?"

"Him and the other two," Spender said. "We can't let him go and not the others. It'll look suspicious."

"Still," Clint said, "you're going to have to get the commissioner's okay on letting them go," Clint pointed out.

Spender smiled and said, "That's where you come in."

"Me? Why me?"

"Because you're the one who's supposed to be getting everything he wants, right? All you've got to do is explain it to the commissioner, and we're on our way."

"We can't both follow Leo," Clint said. "He'll spot us for sure."

"For one thing," Spender said, "he's a drunk, and for another we won't both follow him. I'll follow him, and you follow me."

Clint thought that over for a moment, then said, "That would work."

"I'll wait here while you get it past Commissioner Karl."

"And what about your chief?"

"You'll have to get the commissioner to handle that, too, while you're at it," Spender said. He sat back, grinning broadly. "Good luck."

"I'm going to need it," Clint said.

THIRTY-EIGHT

"You want to let these men go?" George Karl asked, incredulously.

"It's the only way, George," Clint said. "Spender and I have looked at this every way possible. This Leo has to know more than he's telling. We need to be able to follow him."

"What about the other two?"

"We can't let Leo go and not the other two. It will look suspicious."

"How do you plan to follow him?" Karl asked. "You don't know the city. He'll lose you within three blocks."

"I'm not going to follow him," Clint explained. "Spender will, and I'll follow Spender. He won't be trying to lose me."

Karl sat behind his desk, shaking his head.

"Clint, this is the closet we've gotten to finding the killer. In fact, we may have found him. If Leo has been doing the killing and selling the bodies, then we've got him. Why let him go?"

"First of all we can't prove Leo killed anyone," Clint said, "and second, if he has, he's done it for someone else. Don't you want to find the man behind all this? The one buying the bodies?"

"Of course I do," Karl said, "but the mayor already knows we have these three men. If we let them go, and lose them—"

"Why don't we do this?" Clint suggested. "We'll let all three go, but have the other two followed and picked up again right away. We just want Leo to see that he's not the only one being let go."

Karl digested that and then said, "All right, that makes sense. But if you and Spender lose Leo—"

"We won't," Clint said. "Do we have your okay to let them go?"

Karl hesitated, then said, "I ought to have my head examined, but all right. Do it—but if the Mayor finds out—"

"Remind him that he told you to give me anything I want," Clint said. "Oh, and you'll have to explain this to your chiefs."

"Get out of here before I change my mind," Karl said.

Clint got out.

Clint and Spender were across the street when Leo and his two colleagues came out of the police station. The injured man had been seen by a doctor and was limping badly. It would not be difficult to pick him up again.

"If they stay together we might have a problem," Spender said.

"Maybe not," Clint said. "If they stay together they'll have to move at the speed of the slowest man. We'll be able to follow better."

"Doesn't matter," Spender said. "Look, they're arguing. They don't want any part of Leo, and he doesn't want any part of them."

True enough. The three men argued some more, and then Leo waved at them in disgust and walked away. The other two went the opposite way, which was good. Two policemen came out of the building after them, and would pick them up again in a matter of minutes.

"All right," Spender said. "Just stay about a half a block behind me and he won't see you."

"Just make sure he doesn't see you," Clint said.

"I've done this before, Clint," Spender said. "He won't see me."

"Good luck."

Spender nodded, and started after Leo. Clint gave him his half a block, and then followed.

Leo couldn't understand why they'd let him go, but he didn't care. What he needed to do now was get out of town before they came looking for him again. Before he could do that he needed money—and he knew where to get it.

What the doctor and his big servant didn't know was that Leo had followed them one night, after selling them the very first body. Leo wasn't about to do business with anyone without knowing where to find them if he needed to. He knew just where the doctor's clinic was, and he knew his name—Dr. Henry Cecil. He didn't know the big man's name, but that didn't matter. All he'd need to handle him was a gun.

So, first he had to get a gun, and then he'd go to the clinic and get some money off the doctor. He was sure the doctor would pay rather than have Leo give his name to the police.

And he'd pay big.

THIRTY-NINE

Henry Cecil was upset. There was a dead woman in his bed, and this was not the time for this to have happened.

Last night had been a disaster, and he'd had Dimitri dispose of the subject much earlier than he had ever done before. Then he'd gone home and found Elvira waiting for him in bed. He anticipated a long, exhausting night with her after the catastrophe with the new subject, to help get his mind off it, but had quickly discovered that he could not perform. No amount of encouragement from Elvira's mouth or body could bring a reaction from him. He had become angry, at himself, at the subject, and at Elvira for not being able to help him. The last thing he remembered was going to the closet for a whip, and some restraints . . .

He woke up with a dead woman in his bed, and what was worse, there was no thrill at having killed her.

He got dressed and went downstairs to await Dimitri's arrival with the carriage, to take him to the clinic. He would have to decide what to do with Elvira later. Today he had to try to make up for yesterday, and that meant finding another subject—and that meant meeting with the grave digger again.

Life was very hard, sometimes . . .

• • •

Leo considered himself a thorough man. For this reason he had made sure that he not only knew where Henry Cecil's clinic was, but where the man lived, as well. Figuring that the doctor would be at the clinic, Leo—after buying a gun from an acquaintance who assured him it would fire at least twice before exploding in his hand—went to the doctor's home. He figured that before even bracing the man for money, maybe he'd be able to find some in his house. After all, if he didn't have to face the doctor and his man—even with a gun—it would be much better.

Spender couldn't believe it. He'd followed Leo to this house in Cleveland Heights—a house he knew belonged to . . . holy shit! Elvira's doctor friend. *Doctor* Henry Cecil! This was the doctor who was buying dead bodies? How much of a coincidence was *this?*

Clint came behind him, because Leo had broken into the house.

"What's going on?" he asked, crouching behind some brush with Spender.

"I know this house, Clint," Spender said. "It belongs to a doctor named Henry Cecil."

"How do you know that?"

"I can't tell you that, right now," Spender said. "I just do. Take my word for it."

"What kind of doctor is he?"

"I'm not sure," Spender said, "but my information is that he has a clinic, but no patients."

"No live patients," Clint said.

"He must not be home, if Leo figures it's safe to break in."

"He's probably looking for money so he can leave town," Clint said. "Better to steal it than have to ask for it."

"The gun," Spender said. "That's why he bought the gun, in case he has to blackmail the doctor."

Spender wondered whether Elvira had left the house or not. If she was inside . . .

"I have to go in."

"Why not wait until he comes out?" Clint asked. "We can follow him to the clinic."

Spender turned and faced Clint.

"Look, I can tell you where to find the clinic. You go there, and I'll go in the house. Let's see what we each find."

"Eddie," Clint asked, "why is it so important that you go into the house?"

"Clint . . . there's someone I . . . I care about who might be in there. I've got to check."

"We're talking about a woman, right?"

"Yes."

"And she might be in the house?"

"Yes."

"Being held by the doctor, you mean?"

"No," Spender said, "not exactly . . . look, I can't explain it to you now. You have to trust me. Go to the clinic, maybe you'll find Dr. Cecil there—but you'll have to be careful . . . oh Jesus."

"What?"

Spender just realized who the big man was, the one they had arrested at the theater. It was Dimitri. Elvira had told him about the big man, Cecil's assistant and bodyguard. It was all falling into place now. Dimitri made the pickups of the bodies from Leo.

"Eddie?"

"This is it, Clint," he said. "I'm sure of it. Go to the clinic, but watch for Cecil's man. His name is Dimitri, he's the big man from the theater."

"The big man—the same one who has been buying the bodies from Leo?" Clint asked.

"I believe so," Spender said. "We have to split up. We don't know if Cecil's going to want another body today. He got rid of Rachel much quicker than he usually does."

"All right," Clint said, "I'll go, but be careful in there.

Maybe there's more than Leo to worry about."

"I'll go in," Spender said, "check on my friend and join you at the clinic."

"All right," Clint said, putting his hand on Spender's arm. "I don't know what's going on with you, Eddie, but good luck."

"To you, too."

Spender gave Clint precise directions to the clinic, and then Clint turned and walked away, but looked back to see Spender approaching the house. For a moment he thought about following him, but Spender was right. Cecil might be looking for another body today. If he couldn't find Leo and the other grave diggers would he and his man go out looking for themselves?

Clint turned and walked away from the house. He had to put Spender out of his mind, for now. Whatever was going on with him was his business. Right now he had to try to do what he'd promised George Karl he would do.

Suddenly, he couldn't wait to get away from Cleveland. From this point on he could see nothing good happening for him in this city.

FORTY

Leo didn't find any money downstairs so he went upstairs. When he entered the doctor's bedroom he stopped short and stared. The woman on the bed was naked, and there were welts all over her body. Some of them had oozed blood out onto the sheets. He didn't know for sure that she was dead until he approached the bed and saw her face. Her tongue was swollen and protruding from her mouth, and her eyes were open. Even with the swollen tongue he could recognize her, though. The whore, Elvira.

Jesus, he thought, Spender's girl.

He heard something behind him and turned quickly. Standing in the doorway was Detective Spender. He wasn't looking at Leo, though, he was looking at the woman on the bed.

"Jesus, Spender," Leo said, "I didn't do it."

"That sonofabitch," Spender said.

"That's right," Leo said, "he did it, the doc. He's the one. And I'll tell you something else, he's the one's been buying the bodies from me. You musta followed me here. Pretty smart. Well, I can tell ya where he is now. I can tell ya where the clinic is. I just need some money, Spender, to get out of town . . . Spender!"

Spender moved much too quickly for Leo to even have

time to react. Before the skinny grave digger had a chance
to move Spender had him by the throat.

"You sonofabitch!"

"No, not me, Spender," Leo croaked. "Him, the doctor."

"Leo," Spender said, "you're going to tell me everything
I need to know to justify me killing that sonofabitch when
I see him. Understand? I'm going to kill him and get away
with it, and you're going to help me."

"Sure, Spender, sure," Leo said, "anything you say."

Clint followed Spender's directions and found himself
standing across the street from the clinic. From where he
was he could see a shingle on the wall with Dr. Henry Cecil
written on it. Now he had to figure out how to handle this.
He couldn't just walk up to the door and ask the doctor if
he was buying dead bodies, could he? Maybe he could
cross over and get a look inside. The building looked to be
all on one floor, and was actually a home rather than a
clinic. Cecil had probably bought it and turned it into a
clinic. Clint decided to cross over and see if he could get
a look inside a window.

"We would have to go to the cemetery and look for them,
Doctor," Dimitri said. This was in reply to Cecil's question
about where they could find the grave digger, Leo, and
his . . . colleagues.

"Well then, bring the carriage around, Dimitri," Cecil
said. "I need another subject and I need it today."

"But Doctor," Dimitri said, "that's dangerously close to
the other—"

"I'm aware of the risks, Dimitri," Cecil said. "Just do as
I say and get the carriage, like a good man."

"Yes, sir."

Dimitri headed for the front door while Cecil went back
into the laboratory.

•   •   •

Clint was trying to see in a front window when he heard the front door opening. Since the windows seemed to be blocked, keeping him from seeing inside, his only other way to see in was the door. He hurried to the end of the building so he could peer around the wall and possibly get a look inside while not being seen himself. What he saw was the big man from the theater coming out the front door. He left the door slightly ajar and walked down the path to the street, then turned left. As Clint watched, crouched behind some brush now, the man walked to another path that led around to the back of the building.

He didn't know where the big man was going or when he'd be back, but he knew one thing. He had to get inside the building.

He left the safety of the brush and approached the front door.

Clint entered the house and found himself in a large entry foyer. Thankfully, it was empty. He was careful to leave the door ajar exactly as he had found it.

Okay, he was inside. Now what? What were the chances he'd find a dead body someplace in the house? What could he do when he came face-to-face with the doctor? Pull out his badge and arrest him? For what? Shoot him down? How could he justify that, unless the man came at him with a gun?

While he was standing in the entry hall reviewing his options the decision was made for him. A door opened at the end of a hall and a man came walking out. He made a striking appearance for the simple reason he was incredibly ugly. He was short, stocky, walked with a bit of a limp, or a shamble. As he got closer Clint could see that one eye seemed to be set higher than the other, and his nose was misshapen. He was dressed to go out for the afternoon. Clint held his ground and decided to brazen it out. After all, it did say outside that this was a clinic, right?

•   •   •

Dimitri hitched the horse up to the carriage and drove it around to the front of the house. A very meticulous man—when he wasn't being as foolish as he had been at the theater—he noticed that the door was not quite as ajar as he had left it. The difference was minute, but it was there.

He opened the door and stepped in.

FORTY-ONE

When Henry Cecil came out of his laboratory, ready to go out and arrange for his next "subject" he stopped short when he saw the man standing just inside the front door.

"Hello," he said, coming down the hall. "Can I help you?"

"It says outside that this is a clinic?"

"Well, yes . . ."

"And you're the doctor?"

"That's right."

"Well, I'm having this problem—"

"I'm afraid you've come to the wrong place."

"You did say you were a doctor, right?"

"That's right, but—"

"Well, I've got this pain—"

"I'm sorry," Cecil said. "I'm not that kind of doctor."

"What kind of doctor are you?"

"This is a research clinic," Cecil said. "I do not see patients. You'll have to leave—"

"I thought all doctors saw patients," Clint said, stalling for time. If he stalled long enough would something happen? Maybe Spender would arrive and have enough evidence to arrest Cecil.

"I'm afraid I'm going out for the afternoon," Cecil said

167

to Clint. He was pulling on what looked liked expensive calfskin gloves. It was amazing that he could even be a doctor, because each one of his fingers looked like a blunt instrument. "You'll have to find yourself another doctor."

"Can you recommend—" Clint was saying, but the door opened and a man stepped in, cutting him off. He turned and saw the big man who had caused all the commotion at the theater.

"I know you," the man said, pointing his finger at Clint.

Clint had two options that he could see. Shoot them both now or get out of there.

"I don't think so," he said, then turned to the doctor. "Sorry to have bothered you. I'll go and find another doctor."

He turned to leave and Dimitri blocked his way.

"I know him, Doctor," Dimitri said. "He was at the theater the other night. He's a policeman."

"A policeman?" Cecil repeated.

"I'm not a policeman—" Clint said, but Dimitri insisted.

For once in his life Clint Adams moved too slowly. By the time he decided he'd better draw the New Line from his belt Dimitri closed the distance between them in one huge stride and grabbed him by the right wrist.

"What's going on here?" Cecil demanded. "Who are you?"

"He arrested me at the theater," Dimitri said.

"Arrested? You were arrested, Dimitri?"

"It was nothing," Dimitri said. "A misunderstanding."

"A misunderstanding that led him here?" Cecil demanded. "You idiot!"

"No," Dimitri said, "he did not follow me."

"Look, fellas—" Clint said, moving his left hand around behind him. Dimitri was holding his right arm up and was so much taller than Clint that Clint had to stand on his toes. Dimitri saw what he was doing and yanked up on his right arm. The pain was tremendous. Clint felt as if his shoulder was being pulled from the socket. He continued to try and reach around for the New Line with his left hand, but Dimitri saw what he was doing and grabbed the left arm, as well.

"He has a gun," he said.

Cecil stepped forward and while Dimitri held Clint up on his toes the doctor patted him down, found the New Line and removed it.

"This is bad, Dimitri," Cecil said, "very bad. How did you find me, sir?" he demanded of Clint.

"I was told where to come," Clint said, "by a grave digger."

"Grave digger?" Cecil frowned at the reply. "Impossible."

"No, it's not," Clint said. "His name is Leo, and he told us where to find you. In fact, he's in your house, right now."

"My house?" Cecil bellowed. "Someone is in—that *filthy* man is in my house?"

"Right now—"

Dimitri yanked on Clint's arms and now both shoulders felt like they'd been dislocated.

Where the hell was Spender when he needed him?

Cecil went through Clint's pockets and came up with the badge Karl had given him.

"Okay," Clint said, since the doctor had come up with the badge, "now you're both under arrest."

FORTY-TWO

"Dimitri," Henry Cecil said, "I think we should take Mr. Adams into the laboratory."

"Yes, sir."

"I will close the front door and be right with you."

Dimitri nodded and half carried Clint down the hall to the door he'd seen Cecil come out of. The doctor was right behind them after closing and, presumably, locking the front door.

He moved ahead of them, unlocked the door, and led the way in. For some reason, Clint found the temperature in the room cooler. Once he was half carried, half dragged into it Dimitri finally released him. He immediately brought his right hand back to throw a punch at Dimitri, but the arm just flopped at his side. His gun hand and arm were totally useless, and the left was little better.

Where the hell was Spender?

"Dimitri," Cecil said, having removed his coat, but not his gloves, "take Mr. Adams over to the table."

Dimitri advanced on Clint, who braced for the pain when the man grabbed his arm. Instead, Dimitri took him by the collar and propelled him toward the table. It was an odd table, seemingly made of steel, with trenches all around it which all led to a hole at the bottom. Beneath the hole was an empty bucket. The room had the smell of death in it, like a field hospital in a war.

"Mr. Adams—yes, you see, I've figured out who you are. The newspapers were nice enough to put your name on the front page. Well, not your name, but the 'Gunsmith,' but it's the same thing, isn't it? You see, I remember you from your trip to my country, and now you've come along at a very opportune time. You see, I was in need of another subject, and here you are."

"Subjects?" Clint asked. "Is that what you call the people you kill?"

"Kill? Have I killed anyone? I think not, sir."

"All right, then, you have them killed for you," Clint said. "In my book that still makes you a murderer." The feeling was starting to return to his arm.

"Murderer," Cecil said, shaking his head, giving Clint a look one might give to a small child, "this is what you call a man who could change the course of mankind?"

"I don't care what you think your experiments will accomplish, *Doctor*," Clint said, "It doesn't change the fact that you're a murderer."

Cecil shook his head vigorously now and said, "Your opinion. That will change when I make the world aware of my findings."

"Your findings?" Clint asked, flexing his fingers behind his back. "What do you think you're accomplishing here? Working on dead bodies?"

Cecil moved closer to Clint, close enough so that Clint could feel his hot breath, and said, "I will prove that death is not final, Mr. Adams. What do you think of that?"

"I think," Clint said, "that you're a madman."

"Dimitri," Cecil said, "tie Mr. Adams to the table."

Clint kicked out immediately, catching Cecil right in the stomach. The doctor staggered back, all the air driven from his lungs, and sat down on the floor. Clint jumped off the table and backed away as Dimitri came toward him. He knew Cecil had his New Line in his belt, but he couldn't get to the fallen doctor.

The big man continued to advance on him as Clint tried to shake all the feeling back into his arms. The left felt strong enough, but the right was still weak. Still, if he could get to the gun in Cecil's belt he could use it left-handed.

"You kept me from Grace," Dimitri said to him. "Now you will pay."

"Jesus," Clint said, "you're as nuts as he is."

Dimitri charged him and Clint ducked out of the way and ran over to where Cecil was now curled up on the floor. The doctor had curled himself into a fetal position, and he was lying on the gun. Clint tried to roll him over, but his right arm wasn't strong enough. He looked up just as Dimitri reached him. The big man's hand closed on his right shoulder, instantly causing pain. Dimitri lifted him and threw him across the room. Clint slammed into the door and slid down to the floor. At that moment, as Dimitri stalked across the room to him, a murderous look on his face, the door started to open, then stopped when it banged into Clint.

Spender had to kick in the front door of the clinic to get in. He stormed into the house, gun drawn. He wanted to shout out Cecil's name, but didn't want to warn the doctor that he was coming. He looked in the rooms off the foyer, found them empty. There was a hallway leading off to a single door at the end. He started down the hall and as he did something heavy struck it from the other side. He ran to it, tried to open it, but there was an obstruction on the other side. He put his shoulder into it, but it wouldn't budge. He was about to try again when the door suddenly swung open and two huge arms came out, grabbed him, and pulled him in.

Dimitri reached Clint, grabbed him, and moved him out of the way. Clint rolled over and watched as Dimitri knocked

Spender's gun out of his hand. Cecil was still curled up on the floor, obviously not at all used to having violence visited upon his person.

Clint's own breath was coming with difficulty as he watched Dimitri grab Spender by the throat and lift him off the floor.

"You kept me from Grace!" the big man roared. Clint didn't even know if he could tell Spender from Clint, or thought it was the same man. He shook Spender, whose punches were bouncing off of him ineffectually.

Clint crawled across the floor to Cecil, who was still lying on the New Line. That was when he saw the cutdown Colt lying on the floor, where it had skidded beneath the metal table.

Across the room stranger sounds were coming from Spender's throat as Dimitri strangled him. Clint staggered to his feet, fell to his knees, then half staggered, half crawled to the table. He tried to reach for the gun with his right hand, but there was no strength there. Instead, he picked up the gun with his left, then turned and pointed it at Dimitri.

"Put him down, Dimitri!" he shouted.

In his rage Dimitri must have been deaf. Clint pulled the trigger once, a warning shot, but not even that could penetrate the purple and red haze of rage that had fallen over the big man.

Spender began to croak something, his eyes bugging out as he looked across the room at Clint. Finally, Clint made out what he was trying to say.

"Shoot . . . him . . ."

Clint lowered the gun and shot Dimitri in the hip. The bullet smacked into the big man's flesh, blood exploded from the hip, but he did not release his hold on Spender, whose face was beginning to turn purple. Clint shot Dimitri in the knee, then in the side. The big man staggered finally, and dropped Spender to the floor. He turned and charged at Clint, who fired again, and again, and then dropped the hammer on the empty chambers of the gun a few times.

The last two shots punched into Dimitri's chest, one of them exploding his heart. His momentum carried him on toward Clint, who moved out of the way and watched as Dimitri collapsed onto the steel table. It got quiet in the room as he and Spender both tried to catch their breath, along with the wheezing Dr. Henry Cecil. On the table the blood began to seep from Dimitri's wounds into the trenches on the table, where it continued on toward the hole, and then down into the bucket audibly.

Clint cleared his throat and said, "So that's what that's for."

Spender took a long, shuddering breath and found he was finally able to breathe. He got to his feet slowly and walked over to where Clint was sitting on the floor, next to the table. He took a moment to make sure Dimitri was dead, then took the gun from Clint's hand, ejected the empty shells, and then began to reload it.

"What . . ." Clint started, then stopped and tried again. "What . . . happened to Leo?"

"He's in custody again," Spender said. He'd been inches away from killing the man, but hadn't.

"And . . . your friend? The woman?"

Spender looked at him.

"She's dead," he said, then looked at Cecil. "This sick bastard killed her."

With that he walked over to where Cecil was just beginning to unfurl. He saw Spender coming toward him with murder in his eyes and the gun in his hand and held his hands out to ward him off.

"Wait . . . wait . . ." he croaked, ". . . I'm going to save mankind."

"Not today," Spender said.

FORTY-THREE

It was actually several days later before Clint saw Eddie Spender again. First, he spent the morning having breakfast with George Karl after having spent the night saying good-bye to Sherrill. They had been very careful about his right shoulder, which had indeed been dislocated. He was still wearing a sling, and was eating eggs and ham left-handed. No steak. It would have been too hard to cut it.

"The mayor is very happy," Karl said, "the city is happy, and I'm happy. Leo is in jail, Dimitri and Henry Cecil are dead, and there will be no more killings in the name of humanity."

"Oh, here," Clint said. He reached into his pocket, took out his badge, and put it on the table. "This is yours."

"And this," Karl said, taking out a white envelope and putting it on the table, "is yours."

"What's that?"

"Your salary for the time you were a member of my department."

"I wasn't supposed to be on salary."

"I know."

"All my expenses were covered."

"I know," Karl said, "but I told the mayor we owed you something."

"George—"

"Take it," Karl said. "It's from the city of Cleveland, as thanks."

Clint opened his mouth to refuse, then thought better of it.

"Is it in cash?"

"Yes."

He reached for the envelope with his left hand and stuck it into his pocket. He had use for it.

"You know it wasn't me, George," Clint said. "I'm not the hero."

"You are to the city of Cleveland."

Clint had seen the newspapers the next day, announcing that the hiring of the Gunsmith had paid instant dividends as he had brought the killers to justice.

"George—"

"Don't say it, Clint," Karl said, holding up his hand. "I did everything I could for Spender. The fact that he was leading a second life, living with a whore, maybe planning to take down some rich doctor—"

"Dr. Cecil," Clint said, "remember him?"

"That was just a coincidence," Karl said. "It could have been anyone."

"You know, Spender didn't have to tell you what he and the woman were planning."

"I know it."

"You hired him."

"Don't remind me."

"*He's* the hero here, not me."

Karl just stared at Clint, who pushed his plate away and picked up his coffee cup.

"Can I have Hedges take you to the train station?" Karl asked.

"No," Clint said, "I've got a ride."

"I won't ask with who."

Karl stood up and stuck out his left hand. Clint put the cup down to shake it.

"No matter what you say, you helped me out when I needed it," Karl said. "Thanks."

"Good luck, George," Clint said. "I mean, in getting where you want to get to."

"Wherever that is," Karl said. "Thanks, Clint."

Karl walked out of the dining room. When he was gone Clint took out the envelope and counted the money. Twenty-five hundred dollars. A decent amount. He put it back in his pocket.

He called the waiter over and ordered another pot of coffee and an extra cup. Then he settled down to wait.

About fifteen minutes later Eddie Spender appeared in the dining room doorway. He spotted Clint and came walking over.

"Ready?"

"Almost," Clint said. "Sit down and have some coffee. We've got time before the train leaves."

Spender sat down and poured some coffee.

"How's the arm?"

"It's okay," Clint said. "I'll probably take the sling off when I get to the train."

"Wouldn't want to sit on the train looking like a target."

"That's the idea."

While Spender sipped his coffee Clint took out the envelope and put it in the center of the table.

"What's this?"

"Take a look."

Spender did, taking the time to count the money without taking it out of the envelope.

"What's this for?"

"You don't have a job," Clint said. "You need a bit of a cushion until you can find something."

Spender dropped the envelope back on the table.

"I look like a charity case to you?"

"It's not my money."

"Whose is it?"

"The city of Cleveland."

Spender didn't hesitate.

"I'll take it," he said, and tucked the money away in his own pocket. "I'm gonna go private, open my own office."

"In Cleveland?" Clint asked.

"Why not?" Spender asked. "This is the city I know, this is where my contacts are. I can become Cleveland's Talbot Roper."

"There are worse things to be," Clint said.

They sat in silence for a few moments before Clint broke it.

"I'm sorry about Elvira," he said. They hadn't seen each other since that day, and this was his first chance to express his sympathy.

"I knew it couldn't last," he said. "I don't know what I was doing in that relationship. We were each in a business where one of us could end up dead."

More silence, broken by Spender.

"I owe you, Clint."

"You were the one who came busting in and saved my life," Clint reminded him.

"You were the one who kept Dimitri from strangling me to death," Spender said. "I think we're pretty even on that count."

"Okay," Clint said, "so we're even."

"No," Spender said, "you know what I mean. I killed Henry Cecil in cold blood. If you hadn't lied, I'd be in jail right now."

"Cecil deserved to die," Clint said. "He was a sick man."

"You know," Spender said, "there are those in favor of helping sick men like him, rather than putting them away or executing them."

"Well," Clint said, "luckily none of those people are at this table."

"And none of them were in that clinic."

"Right."

They sat quietly for a few moments more and then Clint

gingerly removed his arm from the sling and tried out his hand.

"Looks better," Spender said.

"Much."

Clint removed the sling and laid it aside.

"Ready to leave Cleveland?" Spender asked.

"Eddie," Clint said, pushing his chair back, "I've never been more ready to leave a city in all my life."

J. R. ROBERTS
THE GUNSMITH

Prices slightly higher in Canada

Explore the exciting Old West with one of the men who made it wild!